May 12, 1816
London

Dear Mary,

I am flying to send this off by the next packet. I have a very special plea. Daniel's uncle, Capt. Frank Hodge of the Royal Navy, is in Halifax while his frigate, the Comfort, *is being refitted. Now that the war is over he will be returning to England this fall. On his way he is to stop in New York for provisions. As a very special favor to his sister, Daniel's mother, Captain Hodge has agreed to carry you to London. Mary, please come. I promise to show you all the glories of London. . . .*

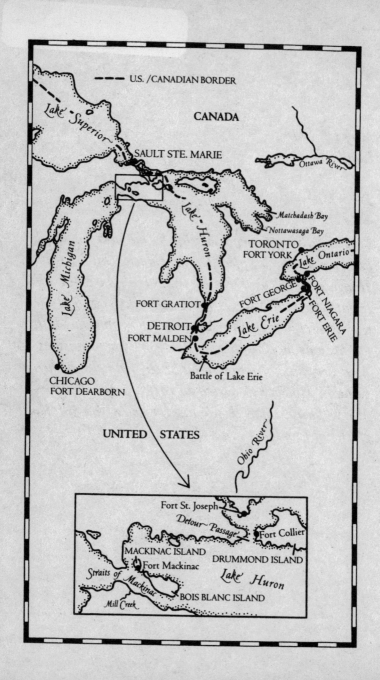

FAREWELL TO THE ISLAND

GLORIA WHELAN

HarperTrophy®
A Division of HarperCollins*Publishers*

Farewell to the Island
Copyright © 1998 by Gloria Whelan
All rights reserved. No part of this book may be used or reproduced in any manner
whatsoever without written permission except in the case of brief
quotations embodied in critical articles and reviews. Printed in the United States
of America. For information address HarperCollins Children's Books, a division of
HarperCollins Publishers, 10 East 53rd Street, New York, NY 10022.

Library of Congress Cataloging-in-Publication Data
Whelan, Gloria.
     Farewell to the island / Gloria Whelan.
          p.   cm.
     Summary: In 1816, sixteen-year-old Mary O'Shea accepts her married sister's
invitation to visit her in London and experiences much of the world beyond her
beloved family farm on Mackinac Island.
     ISBN 0-06-027751-3. — ISBN 0-06-440821-3 (pbk.)
     [1. Family life—Michigan—Mackinac Island (Mich. : Island)—Fiction.
2. Farm life—Michigan—Mackinac Island (Mich. : Island)—Fiction.
3. Mackinac Island (Mich. : Island)—Fiction.   4. London (England)—Fiction.]
I. Title.
PZ7.W5718Far   1998   98-16089
[Fic]—dc21   CIP
                                                                          AC

Typography by Christine Kettner
❖
First Harper Trophy edition, 1999

Visit us on the World Wide Web!
http://www.harperchildrens.com

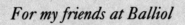

For my friends at Balliol

CHAPTER

1

ON THE FIRST DAY of May, a flimsy snow
fell on our island of Michilimackinac. With the
west winds blowing in from Lake Michigan, and
the east winds blowing in from Lake Huron, we
never knew what would fall from the sky. The
violets my sister, Angelique, had transplanted
from the woods to our garden poked up, making
lavender and purple blotches in the snow. I
thought of the violets we had scattered over her
wedding cake the summer before, the summer

of 1815, when she married her British soldier. Now Angelique was in England, thousands of miles away from our island farm and from Papa and me.

Angelique had married the enemy, for we had been at war with England when she fell in love with Daniel Cunningham. Papa, who had fought with the American army, had gritted his teeth at the horrible thought of an English son-in-law. It was only when he saw that Daniel did not have horns and a tail, and was very nice besides, that he gave his permission for the marriage.

Nine long months had passed since Angelique and Daniel had sailed for England. I knew Papa missed Angelique as much as I did, but he said I must stop moping and think of making my new sister welcome. I meant to do my best, but I was sure Little Cloud could never take Angelique's place. Little Cloud is the daughter of a Sauk chief, so I suppose she is a kind of princess. She and my brother had been engaged for a year. Fur traders like my brother, Jacques, often took Indian brides. The traders might live with the same tribe for many months of the year, and their Indian wives would teach them the language and customs of the tribe. But Jacques had told me that was not the only reason he wished to marry Little Cloud. He confessed that he did indeed love her.

For myself, I had fits of puzzlement as to how I was to act with my princess sister-in-law. Of course she would be welcome, but our life here would surely be different from her life with her own tribe. Her tribe had thousands of acres of woods and water for their home. We have only an island so small that if you climb a hill you can see from one shore to the other. Jacques would be little help in making his new bride feel at home on our farm. I loved my brother dearly, but he was always rushing from one thing to the next with never a look over his shoulder. His heart was not in farming, but far in the west with the fur traders.

Papa and I first learned of Jacques and Little Cloud's coming only a week before from a trader who had stopped at Michilimackinac. He had seen my brother making his way across Lake Michigan. Jacques had asked the trader to bring us the news of his marriage and to tell us that he would be home the first week of May with his new wife. Papa had seemed pleased at the news. I believe he thought Jacques might settle down now that he was married. But I was not so sure.

Papa and I worked hard to get our small

house ready for Jacques's return. Papa gave the walls of the cabin a new coat of whitewash. I laundered the blue-and-yellow calico curtains and beat the sand from the rugs, which had been braided by my mother. She had died sixteen years before, in 1800, the year I was born. Because I could not remember my mother, Angelique had been as much a mother to me as a sister, so I missed her twice as much.

With Angelique gone I was in charge of the house. Papa gave me what little money was needed to walk to the village store for flour or salt. When money was scarce, as it often was, the store took eggs or Belle's milk in trade. I managed the cooking and cleaning, the chickens and the milking. Papa took care of the hogs, cut wood, and did stonework for our neighbors on the island. We tended the crops together. I hoped Little Cloud liked housework and cooking, for I hated it. Instead I longed to be outdoors—in the woods tracking wolves, or running along the sandy shore of the island scaring up gulls or looking for eagles.

Yet, for all the work I had to do, I did not wish to be any place in the world but our island. For the three years that the British soldiers occupied our island—years when Papa was gone—I had kept our farm going. Our farm became more dear to me every day. I could not ask for anything better than to live there with Papa forever.

I had just rolled up my sleeves to make Papa's favorite potted hare from a pair of rabbits he had shot, when the door burst open. I felt myself caught up and swung around in a circle. "Jacques!" I cried. I threw my arms around my brother and hugged him until he begged to be free.

"Mary! Let me go! You are worse than a grizzly bear."

Jacques had grown to be taller than Papa. He was less like a sapling and more like a sturdy tree. "What is that thing on your upper lip?" I teased. "The scraggly tail of some animal, surely!"

"Never mind that. Just tell me how your hair could have gotten even redder. It looks like a stew of carrots."

When I could take my eyes from Jacques I saw Papa standing at the door, his arm around an Indian girl. Her long black hair hung in a thick braid over her shoulder. Her skin was golden and she had the kind of high cheekbones that my round face would never have. She wore a deer-skin dress trimmed with fringe and embroidery. I thought her very beautiful. I believe Papa did too, for his face was full of happiness and pride. The last time I had seen so much pleasure on his face was on his return to the island last summer after his long absence. Then his smiles had all been for me, for taking such good care of the farm.

Angry with myself for my jealous thoughts, I went at once to embrace Little Cloud. She looked frightened, though, and drew away from me.

"Don't try one of your bear hugs on Little Cloud," Jacques said. "She isn't used to all that squeezing from strangers. If she could speak our language she would tell you it isn't dignified."

I spoke quickly to hide my hurt. "You've been traveling in this snow. Let me get you some warm tea to drink. I have your favorite honey cake, Jacques." In no time we were sitting around the table exchanging stories.

"Wait until you see the pelts we have brought back," Jacques said. "Bearskin, beaver, fisher, lynx, fox, wolf, otter, and mink. That's not even counting all the muskrat we speared after the Rock River froze up and we could get to their huts." I tried not to wince at the thought of Jacques's canoe piled high with the skins of little dead animals.

Jacques told of his travels all the way from the Mississippi. He had tales of tangles with rattlesnakes and of fields full of buffalo, of falling out of his canoe in a rapids and nearly drowning, and of being so hungry he had to chew his shoes for nourishment. Most frightening of all was his narrow escape from the arrows of unfriendly Indians who did not want him trapping on their land. He laughed as he told these stories, so I did not know if they were all to be believed. Yet if these dangers had not befallen him, others surely had, for beneath his laughter and his light ways there was a new calmness and composure. I saw that the difficulties of his travels had seasoned my brother.

Jacques's love for the wilderness shone in all of his words. "Papa, how I wish you and Mary could travel the river with me. On either side of its banks are forests of oak trees that reach nearly to heaven. The branches on one side of the stream stretch across to meet the branches from the other side so that you travel under a leafy canopy. Then suddenly you are in the clear and floating around green islands and between high cliffs. In the evenings we would pull up onto the shore and build a great fire to cook up a little venison or some freshly caught fish. We would fall asleep with no sound but the crackling of the fire, the rush of the river, and a busy owl or two."

As we chattered on, Jacques would turn to Little Cloud with a fond look and translate for her. "She understands some of what we say, for I have taught her a fair amount of English. It is just that she is timid of showing it off. Her English words are as pretty as anything you could wish."

Little Cloud must have understood what Jacques said, for she smiled and shyly lowered her head. Her gestures were so graceful that the coldness that had been growing in my heart melted at once and I thought perhaps she would be like a sister after all.

"Jacques and Little Cloud," Papa said, "after so long a journey you will want to unpack your things and rest a bit before our supper. Mary, it would be generous of you to give them the loft so that they might have a room of their own. You can have my corner of the cabin. I am content to make my bed here by the fire."

"Yes, Papa," I mumbled. "I'll just clear out my things."

I hurried up the ladder so that no one should see my tears. Of course they must have a place to call their own. In all my preparations why had I not thought of that? Perhaps because I could not bear the thought of giving up the loft. It had been my room as long as I could remember. I had shared it with Angelique. When I missed her the most it was where I could go to make her real to me again. From the small window over my bed I looked out at Lake Huron and Lake Michigan as they flowed together to make a watery ring around our island. From the window I was eye to eye with the gulls. It was where I watched the first snow of the year and, at winter's end, the last.

For three years I had watched the British flag fly over our island fort from the window of the loft. A year ago, with the war over, I had seen the American flag returned to its rightful place. When I climbed up the ladder and shut the little door, I was in my own world. Now that world was being taken from me.

I gathered up my few possessions, my two everyday dresses, and the good dress made for Angelique's wedding. I took the little box that held the silver cross I had from Mama and the blue beads given to me by my dearest friend, White Hawk. I looked out the window for the last time. The snow had melted and in the blue sky I saw an eagle, the first of the season, soaring over the island. With that small happiness I had to be content.

At the supper table Little Cloud was puzzled by the knives and forks and spoons. She sat with her hands folded until she saw what we did. Cautiously she followed, but you could see the lesson was not easy for her. The fork and knife did not do quite what she wished. Some of the food I had so carefully prepared was not to her liking. She chewed on the bread with a worried look and seemed puzzled by the blancmange pudding I had taken so much trouble over.

Papa and I were careful not to stare. Jacques did not even seem to notice. As always, he was rushing headlong into a scheme. "Here's what we must do," he said. "We'll invite all the neighbors to come tomorrow to meet Little Cloud. We'll ask the Sinclairs, the MacNeils, the Wests, and Pere Mercier. You can cook up a feast for us, Mary. Papa and I will find you some grouse and rabbits. Little Cloud will come with us, for no one is as clever as she at setting snares for rabbits."

Papa agreed at once. "Pere Mercier has been catching great quantities of whitefish, and he has offered to give some to us. And we have a ham hanging in Mr. MacNeil's smokehouse. I know you will do us proud, Mary."

I saw immediately that instead of having less work, I would have more. Now I would be waiting upon Jacques and Little Cloud as well as Papa. Silently I began gathering up the dishes. Little Cloud started to get up to help me, but Jacques bid her sit down again. As in everything else, to my disgust, she obeyed him. "Let Mary do it," he said. "She likes playing the house-wife."

In the old days I would have pushed him off his chair for such raillery, but now Jacques was a grown man and a husband. So I did not push him, but as I picked up his plate I saw to it that a good bit of gravy got splashed on his shirt. But the best thing that happened all that day was this: As Jacques was making a great fuss about the gravy spot Little Cloud looked up at me, and I saw the tiniest smile steal across her face.

CHAPTER

2

WE WERE A CHEERFUL party the next day. When you live crowded onto a small island you must either love your neighbor or hate your neighbor, and loving is more pleasant. There were warm congratulations for Jacques and Little Cloud, both of whom were looking splendid. Little Cloud was in a deerskin dress trimmed all over with shells. She wore dangling silver earbobs and silver bracelets. Jacques was in a long frock coat of deer hide. The hem of the coat was fringed and the lapels and cuffs were embroidered with flowers. "Little Cloud's work," he said proudly.

To accommodate everyone we had to sit closely around the table. The blacksmith, Angus MacNeil, who shoed horses for the soldiers and was often first to hear any rumor, filled us in on all the news from the fort.

Pere Mercier was eager for news of his friend, Pere Boucher, who had a mission on the Mississippi near the Sauk. It was he who had married Jacques and Little Cloud.

Dr. West rejoiced because Napoleon was safely locked up in St. Helena. Napoleon had stirred up trouble in Europe as if with a great spoon. Everyone was happy his mischief-making was over.

Looking around the table, I caught Mrs. West frowning at our thick, clumsy mugs, which she must have considered unsuitable for guests. In the Wests' home tea was served in china cups as blue and fragile as robins' eggs. Her eldest daughter, Elizabeth, was a year older than Angelique, and had the haughtiness of her mother. She let us see that she was much bored with our company, for we were none of us eligible bachelors.

Elizabeth ignored Little Cloud, treating her

as no more than a savage. But Elizabeth's younger sister, Emma, could not take her eyes from her. Though Jacques had never guessed it, Emma had cared deeply for him. Little Cloud's beauty and Jacques's clear affection for his bride were hard on her. I could not bear to look at Emma for the pain on her face.

But most of my attention was on what the Sinclairs were saying about White Hawk. The Sinclairs had a farm near ours and were step-parents to White Hawk, whom they called Gavin. On a Christmas Eve more than a dozen years ago, Mr. West had been out fishing and was making for shore in a storm when he saw a young Indian boy clinging to a tipped canoe. Mr. Sinclair rescued the boy, whose family had drowned, and took the boy home to raise as his own son. "A Christmas present!" Mrs. Sinclair had said.

White Hawk and I had grown up together. We shared a love for the woods. Whenever we could escape our tasks we were off picking berries or searching for wild honey or looking for the nesting places of eagles. Then one day everything changed. White Hawk learned that his real father had been an Ottawa chief and he left the Sinclairs to join his tribe on the mainland at L'Arbre Croche. Last fall he had gone to Detroit to attend Pere Richard's new school.

"I hope he is keeping up his Latin," Pere Mercier said. "He was my best pupil."

"We have a letter from Pere Richard," Mr. West said. "He has nothing but good things to say of Gavin."

"And Gavin is returning this week," Mrs. Sinclair added. "In time to help Mr. Sinclair with the plowing. How good it will be to have him home."

I did not mention that I had a letter from White Hawk with the same news. I had read and reread the letter a hundred times, hoping that the reading of his words would hurry White Hawk home. I asked, "He won't be going back to his tribe at L'Arbre Croche?" I held my breath.

"Oh, I daresay he'll be back and forth," Mr. Sinclair answered. "After all, they look on him as the man who will be their chief one day. But he promises to come to us first."

To hide my pleasure at the thought of White Hawk's return I set about serving a pound cake, which I had made with no thought to how much butter or how many eggs I was wasting. I put a dollop of wild strawberry jam on each piece. I had been saving that last jar of jam. It was made from berries White Hawk and I had picked together.

After dinner it was time for wedding gifts. "I managed to get a fine bit of iron on the last ship up from Detroit," Mr. MacNeil said, "and I put it to good use." He produced a handsome pair of andirons from his forge. They were shaped like soldiers. "After all, Jacques, while you were not exactly a soldier, you did fight the British."

It was true. When the Americans had marched onto Michilimackinac to try to take the island back from the British, Jacques had joined the battle. White Hawk's tribe was fighting with the British, and White Hawk and Jacques, who had once been best friends, had nearly killed one another. It was that battle that made them decide they were meant to be friends and not soldiers.

For my gift I had hemmed a tablecloth from a fine piece of linen that my mother had brought from France, where she grew up. On each corner of the cloth I had embroidered wildflowers found on our island: daisies, trillium, violets, spring beauties, and goldenrod. I am not clever at fine handwork, so there were many ripped stitches. Still, Little Cloud seemed pleased. She laughed with pleasure as she recognized each flower, asking Jacques to tell me that those flowers also grew in her own land. For the first time I realized that Little Cloud must be homesick.

Mrs. West brought out a small box wrapped in a scrap of velvet. She handed it to Little Cloud, who looked confused, not knowing if the fancy wrapped box was the gift or if there was something more she should do with the box. Jacques gestured that she should open the box. Inside was a china parrot so cleverly painted it looked as if it might speak at any moment. Little Cloud exclaimed with delight and held the bird to her.

When it was the Sinclairs' turn, Mr. Sinclair said, "I'm afraid we have nothing so fine to give, but I hope our gift will be useful. If you will excuse me, I will just go out to get it." A moment later he was back with a squealing piglet that would not be held. The whole party was soon in great confusion as we all dashed about the cabin trying to recapture the pig, who did not intend to give up his first taste of freedom. Only Elizabeth gave no help, standing apart with her silk skirts held close, as if afraid the piglet might rush at her and eat her up.

When the scrambling was over and the pig restored to our pigpen, it was Papa's turn. With great solemnity he handed Jacques a piece of official-looking paper. I saw that Jacques was not anxious to have it in his hand. He read it slowly. The only pleasure on his face was put there for Papa and the company. It did not come from his heart. He looked around at the guests and then, with his smile becoming braver, he said, "Papa has given me our farm."

I could not believe my ears. With a sinking heart I heard Papa say, "I'm getting on in years. Now that he is a settled, married man, it is Jacques's turn. But you need not give up the fur business entirely, Jacques. Mr. Astor plans an office right here on Michilimackinac for his fur company. With your experience as a trader there is no doubt Mr. Astor will find you a position."

The terrible injustice of what Papa had done crushed me. I was too shocked and miserable to join in the rejoicing. I had always believed the farm would be mine. All Jacques had ever wanted was to be a trader tramping about the wilderness. He could not wait to get away from the farm and our island for the west. While the British had occupied Michilimackinac, Jacques had run off with traders, leaving Angelique and me to care for the farm. We had nearly starved. We had beaten off British soldiers by hiding our cow, Belle, in our house. When winter came I tunneled through snow as high as myself to see to Belle. In the summer I worked in our fields all day under hot sun. I had done it all because I loved the farm more than anything in the world. Papa was breaking my heart by giving it to Jacques—who did not even want it.

Papa was taken aback by the storm on my face. "Mary, there is nothing to fret about. You surely know that if something should happen to me, Jacques and Little Cloud will always have a place for you here."

Those words were like poison. I was to be a slave on a farm I would never own, grateful to Jacques and Little Cloud for every bit of food that went into my mouth. I would have run from the room in anger but for Little Cloud's astonishing actions. Her eyes had grown larger and larger with each gift. Now she began pulling the bracelets from her arms and snatching off her earbobs. She moved about the room pressing her silver decorations upon our startled guests. When they would not take them she was puzzled and hurt. When I saw her distress I put aside my own misery. I saw for the first time how strange our customs must seem to Little Cloud. My heart went out to her.

Quickly Jacques put an arm around her. "I

apologize," he said to our guests. "Among Little Cloud's people, if you are given a present you must give back a present of equal or greater value. Her tribe admires people not for the goods they acquire but for their generosity. Let me explain to her what our customs are and I am sure she will be as grateful for your kindness to us as I am."

In all the confusion we had not noticed the door opening. When I happened to look up, there stood White Hawk!

CHAPTER

3

I COULD NOT TAKE my eyes from White Hawk, and I hoped no one noticed. He was taller than I remembered and dressed in his usual fashion of half farmer and half Indian, with corduroy trousers, a deerskin jacket, and a buckskin hat. His long black hair no longer fell loose about his shoulders but hung in two braids wrapped around with bands of fur. I thought the new style quite fetching, but Jacques could not wait to chafe him. He called out, "I suppose you must get up earlier these days to prettify your hair, White Hawk. Next you'll put down your hunting musket for an embroidery needle."

White Hawk only laughed. "I saw the pile of furs you and the Gauthiers brought back. There is no need for anyone to think of taking up a musket to hunt. After your greed there can be no animals left upon the face of the earth. Soon we shall need another Noah's ark." Jacques and White Hawk had been teasing one another since they were children. Although their words were cutting their banter had no sharp edges, for they were the best of friends.

The Sinclairs greeted their adopted son warmly, calling him Gavin. Everyone called him that except for Jacques and myself. As he made the rounds of the guests, I felt the strong pressure of his hand as he greeted me. "Mary O'Shea," he laughed, "you are a young woman and probably too much a lady to chase through the woods with me now."

"Never in the world would I be too much a lady for a romp in the woods," I said with great feeling. Then I saw that White Hawk was no longer listening to me. He was staring at Little Cloud, and the look of fascination on his face chilled my heart.

"Well, Jacques," he said. "How is it that someone so elegant would be willing to marry a clod like you?"

The word *elegant* pierced my soul. Little Cloud with her beauty and quiet ways truly was elegant. It was a word that I knew would never be used to describe me, with my red hair, round face, and unruly ways. If that was what White Hawk wished in a woman, all my hopes were dashed. Had anyone noticed my burning face they would have guessed how much I cared for White Hawk. Fortunately no one was paying me any attention. They all had questions about Detroit.

As he talked of Detroit, White Hawk became somber. "Since the war, life has been very hard for the people in Detroit. The British and the Indians who fought with them did much burning and looting. Many families are grieving for loved ones killed in the war. This winter there were some in the town whose hunger was so great it caused them to boil up hay for their supper. We thought at first there was no hope for crops since all the seed had been stolen or destroyed. Now the government in Washington has sent money to buy new seed and things are looking better.

"For myself, I have no complaints," he continued. "I have been studying with Pere Richard, who is a great teacher. He came to Detroit from France, where the French revolutionaries were chopping off the heads of priests. He has started schools for both Indian and white children. He and Mr. Monteith, a Presbyterian minister, are laboring to start a fine university very like the Sorbonne in France. The Indians have even given Pere Richard some of their land along the Raisin River to be sold to raise money for such a school. One day soon we'll have a university for Michigan and it will be paid for by the Indians."

The rest of the day passed in friendly talk. By the time our neighbors left there wasn't so much as a crumb left on the table. As he said adieu, Pere Mercier, an old fishing companion of Jacques's, offered, "If you can manage to get up at a decent hour, Jacques, I have a *bonne place* for perch." Shaking his hand, Jacques promised that he would do his best.

White Hawk stayed on to exchange stories with Jacques. He also had many questions for Little Cloud. "What do you think of our country?" he asked her.

"It was once her country as well," Jacques said pointedly. "The Sauk lived not far from here until the Iroquois and the French chased them west."

Little Cloud must not have liked Jacques's description of her people being driven off their land, for—using half English and half Indian, which Jacques translated for me—she said, "No one dares fight us now. In our village of Saukenuk there are a hundred lodges along the Mississippi. If anyone should march against us there are a thousand warriors to fight them. We will not give up any more of our land." Her soft voice hardened and she spoke as a chief's daughter.

"I am with you in that!" White Hawk said. He looked at her with admiration. "Here in our Michigan territory Governor Cass has set out to make Michigan a state. For that he wants to take the rest of the Indians' land from them. I mean to stop him!"

So busy were White Hawk and Little Cloud in speaking of the need to defend the land of their people, they took no notice of my slipping out to milk Belle. Belle stretched out her chin, but I had no heart for giving her the scratching she expected. Instead I rested my head against her warm flank as I milked her, and thought of all I had lost. Angelique was thousands of miles away. The loft was no longer mine. The farm was to be Jacques's. And White Hawk seemed much more interested in Little Cloud than in me.

As time went on, things did not get better. There seemed to be nothing in which Little Cloud did not excel. When Jacques returned from a hunting expedition near St. Ignace with several fox skins, Little Cloud set about scraping the skins and stretching them on hoops she fashioned of willow boughs. When the skins were dried she oiled and rubbed them until they were as soft as a baby's skin. With great admiration White Hawk said, "The women of my tribe at L'Arbre Croche are not nearly so clever."

Little Cloud had brought sunflower seeds with her to plant. At first Papa was skeptical. "We can't give over any more of our valuable ground to flowers," he said. But Little Cloud coaxed, "The seeds can be feed for the hogs, and when they are pounded and parched and ground into meal I can make a tasty dish as well."

When it was time to plant our corn, Little Cloud said, "The spring has been so cold we must soak the seed kernels in warm water."

Papa appeared worried. "It's too risky. What if it kills the seeds?"

"Let me try a few kernels," Little Cloud pleaded. At the end of the first week our kernels had not yet sprouted, while Little Cloud's were poking up through the ground. Papa was more pleased than ever that he had given the farm to Jacques and Little Cloud. What he did not see was how homesick Little Cloud was or how hastily Jacques did his work so that he could be off exchanging stories with the fur traders who were arriving each day on the island with their pelts.

As for me, Papa was full of praise for my hard work. He didn't notice how little joy I took in my tasks. I couldn't put my heart into it knowing that the farm was never to be mine.

Now that the British soldiers were gone from our island and the waters of Lake Michigan and Lake Huron were open once more to trade, the Indians were returning to the island. When the time came for the Indians to receive their yearly payment for the land they had sold to the government, there were more than a thousand teepees spread along the shore. The smoke from their campfires hung like lowering clouds over the whole island. The loud rhythm of their drums was like the beating of a great bird's wings.

The drums cheered Little Cloud. "It is like hearing my own heart beating," she said to me. Though the Indians who camped on the island were mainly Ottawa and Ojibwa, their language was much like Little Cloud's. "When I talk to them," she said, "my own voice comes back to me. I don't miss my people so much."

In the evenings Jacques and White Hawk and Little Cloud and I would go down to the Indian camp. The Indians were wonderful to see. Some wore buckskin tunics over their leggings, others topped their leggings with trade blankets or the red jacket of a British soldier. They were adorned with necklaces of silver disks, or coins of copper and brass. Some who had traveled west wore necklaces fashioned out of the claws of a grizzly bear. Their hair was done up in ribbons or turbans or feathers, and for special dances their faces were streaked in blues and yellows and reds. There was so much to catch your eye, you could hardly take it all in.

While I loved to see the splendor of the clothes and watch the dancing, I felt left out. The other three could understand and speak to the Indians, while I could not. Having lived with the Sauk, Jacques had become nearly as clever at the Indian language as White Hawk was. White

Hawk would begin to translate for me, but then he would get lost in some warrior's tale and forget all about me. When I would beg, "What's he saying?" he would only tell me to hush.

After a while I made excuses to stay at the farm, though I found little happiness there. In the past everything I saw as I walked around our property was very dear to me. Now it was all changed. The house I had believed would be mine one day would belong to my brother. The land I had worked all these years was to be his as well. Even my beloved Belle and George, Belle's son, were not mine. George was a fine bull whom I had delivered and but for my efforts would have perished. As I walked across our land I kicked a stone out of the way. Stones were forever shouldering their way out of the earth. The stone fell among the rows of corn. In the past I would have placed it carefully on Papa's stone pile so that he could use it for building. Now I did not care.

CHAPTER

4

JACQUES was no happier than I was. Mr. Jacob Astor was indeed coming to Michilimackinac, just as Papa predicted. "He's going to make a business out of it," Jacques told me. He had been watching the building of what was to be the headquarters of Mr. Astor's American Fur Company.

Papa could no longer ignore Jacques's wish to be a fur trader. Papa thought by urging Jacques to seek a job with Mr. Astor's company, he could keep Jacques on the island and on the farm. Papa said, "Astor is sure to succeed, for since the war only Americans can be licensed to be fur traders. At last we are finished with England's Hudson's Bay Company." Papa had little good to say of the British. He had come to America from Ireland, where the English had settled in like a skunk in a groundhog's burrow. When we were growing up, Papa used to tell us stories of Ireland and its green land and its people who longed to be free of the British.

Finally Jacques gave in. Looking glum and dragging his feet, he made his way into the village and applied to Mr. Astor's company for a job. Jacques was clever at sums, and when he put his mind to it he could write a tolerable hand. He was hired as a clerk.

I heard him complain to White Hawk, "In the fall, instead of setting off for the West, I will sit all day scratching down lists of goods to go to the traders. In the spring I will scratch down the number of pelts the company has collected from the traders. Astor will own all the traders and tell them where to go. It will be no better than horse trading.

"Worst of all, Astor will send his boats out to collect the furs from the trappers. Most of the traders won't come to the island, so I will not even hear of all the adventures I am missing. I will be chained to an office all day and I will hate it. And at night I will be ploughing fields and slopping hogs. I should never have come home."

Of course, all of Jacques's complaints were made out of Papa's hearing, for Jacques did not want to seem ungrateful for the gift of the farm. Still, Jacques's discontent could not be entirely hidden, and Papa became unhappy. With Little Cloud standing each day looking westward toward her home, me kicking stones, Jacques grumbling, and Papa bewildered by his nest of cross-patches, things at home on the island were not very pleasant.

Then Angelique's letter came.

May 12, 1816
London

Dear Mary,

I am flying to send this off by the next packet. I have a very special plea. Daniel's uncle, Capt. Frank Hodge of the Royal Navy, is in Halifax while his frigate, the Comfort, *is being refitted. It was badly damaged in an* engagement with the American navy. Now that the war is over he will be returning to England this fall. On his way he is to stop in New York for provisions, great pine masts or something of that nature to be had only in America. He sails from New York for London in October. As a very special favor to his sister, Daniel's mother, Captain Hodge has agreed to carry you to London. He sails by October 1, so you must be there well in time. It was he who carried Daniel and me back to London and I have never forgotten his kindness.

Mary, please come. I love Daniel very much. He and his family are good to me. But I long to hear about Papa and Jacques and Little Cloud and all of our friends on the island. Papa has written to tell us that Jacques is to have the farm and how well Little Cloud is doing. I am sure with Little Cloud there to help, you would not be too badly missed.

I promise to show you all the glories of London. How they will make you exclaim! I am tres occupé here in London. Much of my time is filled with visiting and balls, but sometimes, on a warm day when the sun shines, we ride in our carriages in Hyde Park, and the sight of the trees and the sound of the *birds makes me long for our island of Michilimackinac.*

You must let me know immediately so that we can get word to Captain Hodge. It is very kind of him to carry you on the Comfort. *Everyone speaks of what a fine naval officer he is. No one has a more orderly ship.*

Daniel wishes to send money for your travel to New York City and your passage. He promises you shall have a horse for your very own to ride.

Give my special love to Papa and Jacques and welcome Little Cloud for me. And, Mary, please do come,

Your loving sister,
Angelique

At any other time I would not have thought of leaving our island. Now I pressed Angelique's letter to my heart. At last I would have someone I could confide in, someone who would understand how I felt about the farm. I had not thought it would ever come to my looking forward to going away.

At first Papa was shocked. "It is bad enough having one of my daughters so far from me." He frowned and added, "And in England at that. Sure, it might be a fine opportunity, but I do not see how I can spare you, Mary."

"But Papa," I pleaded. "The planting is all done. And with Jacques and Little Cloud to help you there is very little for me to do."

Papa did not notice the sulkiness in my voice but only said, "A trip to England would take two or three months. How are we to make arrangements for such a journey?"

Jacques came to my rescue. "Pierre Bonnart is taking a load of furs to Detroit on a sloop. His wife, Marie, will go with him, as she always does. She is as good a sailor as Pierre. From Detroit, Mary can take a schooner across Lake Erie to Buffalo and a stagecoach from Buffalo to Albany. There she can take passage on a steamboat to New York." The thought of all this travel began to frighten me, but then I saw how much Jacques wished he could take such a journey, and I was caught up in his excitement.

Papa said he would think about it, which was very close to a yes.

Later, when we were alone, Jacques said, "If I must stay here, Mary, at least you shall have a chance to escape."

On an island news travels quickly. Soon

everyone knew about my trip. Mrs. West came at once with Emma and Elizabeth. "You will be there just in time for the London season, when all the great balls are held," Mrs. West said. "How I wish my girls could have such an opportunity. No doubt Angelique will find you a suitable husband."

This was more than I could bear. I was looking forward to the adventure, but there was no moment when I did not think I would return to the island. If I thought of a husband at all, my secret thoughts were all of White Hawk. "I have no more need for an English husband than for a pair of antlers or a furry tail," I said firmly.

Elizabeth was seething with jealousy at my trip. She said, "I believe there are as many handsome and well-brought-up girls in London as are needed. I would not think a London gentleman would look to a foreign country girl for a bride."

"Don't be such a snob, sister," Emma said. She turned to me. "Mary, what gowns will you take? I could let you borrow my kid gloves. They come from France, you know."

Mrs. West was equally generous. She gave me a length of muslin for a dress, and kindly brought over women's magazines so that I might choose a fashionable pattern. Even Elizabeth relented in the excitement of the preparations and offered to give me one of her bonnets. "You may take it, Mary. Its pink color is not well with my complexion and the style is last year's."

Since I had so little, I could not be proud. The bonnet was indeed an ugly color, a kind of pig pink. However, I dipped it in blackberry juice to good effect, and the darker shade did not fight with my red hair.

My finest wear came from Little Cloud. I saw her whispering with Jacques and giggling. I caught her poring over the magazines Mrs. West had brought. And for an entire day she hid herself up in the loft.

The evening before I was to leave she and Jacques presented me with a package wrapped in a sheet. I unwound the sheet to find a pelisse made of the silkiest, whitest ermine trimmed with black-tipped ermine tails. The cape fell about my shoulders in the most elegant way. I cried for joy and hugged Jacques and Little Cloud, who by now had grown used to such embraces from me.

"It was Little Cloud's idea that I should save out the ermine we trapped," Jacques said. "She worked with the skins until they were as soft as goose down. Then she copied a picture from one of your silly magazines and stitched the whole thing together."

Later I had the satisfaction of seeing Elizabeth so taken aback, she could not find one unkind word to say about my cape. Instead she asked, "Mother, could we not hire Little Cloud to make a pelisse for us?"

Emma, seeing the furious look on Jacques's face, quickly said, "For shame, Elizabeth. Such skill and love are not to be hired."

I thought Emma's words perfect. And clearly, my brother thought so as well. Her reward was a look of affection from Jacques. For Emma there could be no greater thanks.

The greatest surprise was yet to come. As I was in the midst of packing my trunk, petticoats strewn about the floor and stockings snaking around chairs, White Hawk walked through the door.

"Good heavens, Mary, are you going to London to set up shop? One person could not possibly wear all of that. What's more, your trunk will be so heavy the Bonnarts' sloop will sink to the bottom of Lake Huron and drown both of us."

"What do you mean, 'both of us'? You won't be on it."

"Oh, yes I will. I've had a letter from Pere Richard—classes are about to begin. I've decided to make the voyage to Detroit with the Bonnarts. That way I can keep an eye on you."

A great relief swept over me. With White Hawk at my side for at least a part of the way the journey didn't seem so far. But I did not dare let White Hawk know how pleased I was. To hide my feelings I teased, "I hope when we get to Detroit you will introduce me to Pere Richard, so I can tell him what mischief you get into when you are not under *his* eye."

When it was time to leave, even the prospect of so much time with White Hawk could not keep me from regretting the trip. With all my friends gathered around the pier and with Jacques and Little Cloud looking so sad, I nearly ran up the bluff and back to the farm. It was very foolish of me, but at that moment I would have given anything to throw my arms around Belle.

As they said good-bye to White Hawk, the Sinclairs looked worried. They always did when he left. They were never sure he would return to them.

As Papa embraced me he pressed a five-dollar gold piece into my hand. I remembered how he had trusted me with such a coin when he had left Michilimackinac to fight the British. "A coin like this brought you luck before; let's hope it will bring you luck now." He sighed. "How will we ever get along without you, Mary?" He turned his head so that I could not see his tears. I had welcomed the trip because I was afraid I was no longer needed. Now when it was too late to change my plans I saw that I would be missed after all.

CHAPTER

5

WHEN THE FINAL FAREWELLS were said, Pierre Bonnart cast off, hopping aboard the sloop while Marie set the jib and the mainsail to catch the northwest wind. The little group on the pier grew smaller and smaller until I could barely make out their faces.

In all the excitement of readying for the trip I had not truly realized that I was leaving my island. I had been on canoes and sailboats with Jacques and White Hawk and Papa before—for fishing or pleasure or to cross to the mainland for maple sugaring. But I had never lost sight of the island. I had only to look over my shoulder and there it was, solid as the rocks it was built on.

Now, with a fresh breeze blowing from the northwest, my island was quickly disappearing. I lost heart and began to sob. I was leaving behind everything I cared about, and however hard I tried, I could not see so far as my return.

White Hawk hardly knew what to say to my outbreak. He took my hands in his and tried to comfort me. "Just think, Mary, soon you will be sailing across the ocean to the largest city in the world. When you get back, the island will still be here."

"But so much will have happened by then and I will have missed it all."

It was Marie's sharp voice that helped me to collect myself. "I could use a little help here. Take off those foolish shoes, girl, and wind up this fall of rope. White Hawk, you can stow some of the luggage below."

As I worked at making a neat coil of the ropes I studied the Bonnarts. Pierre was at the tiller, keeping an eye on the top of the mast where a scrap of cloth told the wind's direction. He was as tall and thin as his mast. His face was the color of acorns from being out in all weather. He stared ahead at the great lake, seeming to take pleasure in the miles of empty blue-green. Sometimes his eyes followed the flight of the gulls soaring overhead. He seemed a man who on land had carefully stored up long thoughts to be brought out and examined here on the wide lake, where nothing would disturb him. He was kindness itself when you spoke to him, but his answer always came from a far distance.

Pierre's wife, Marie, was as busy as Pierre was thoughtful. She was like a red squirrel—the littlest of the squirrels, which scurry up and down branches and in and out of holes faster than you can blink an eye. She was small, and her hair was tawny brown. So were her arms and face. While Pierre stared off across the lake, Marie trimmed the sails, did the cooking, rubbed and sluiced the decks clean, and kept up a continual conversation with her passengers. When she was not chattering cheerfully she was shouting "Ready about" or "Helm's alee." At such times we all scrambled to do her bidding. If you did not "look lively," you were in danger of being swept overboard by the heavy boom that swung the sails from port to starboard and back.

Though Marie and Pierre appeared to be very

different, they had a secret way of exchanging thoughts. If the wind changed, a quick look from Pierre to Marie was all that was needed to set in motion the most vigorous hauling on ropes or reefing of sails.

Apart from White Hawk and myself, the only other passengers on board were two traders, a Mr. Creaks and a Mr. Soffle. They had come up from Detroit some weeks before and were now returning. They were as alike as two peas in a pod—short stout men with shifty eyes that would not look at you directly. They were much affected by the sun's heat, mopping their faces and necks with large, checked handkerchiefs. They seldom spoke with us, and talked to one another in a low mumble that could not be over-heard.

When the men were below I asked White Hawk, "Have we seen them before? They look familiar."

"Yes. They were often with the Indians try-ing to interest the chiefs in buying their product. They promised to reward any chief who sup-plied his tribe. When they were not as successful with the chiefs as they'd hoped, they went after the traders, urging them to take their product to the Indians as trade goods."

"What could they be selling? Tools? Guns?"

"They were selling whiskey," he told me disdainfully.

"It's illegal to sell whiskey to Indians! And it's illegal for the traders to offer it in exchange for furs."

"That doesn't seem to trouble our two friends. They are clever at getting around the law. Now they are taking their orders to Detroit, where they will load up and return to Michilimackinac with their poison. I tell you, Mary, for the mischief they make it would be a blessing if they tumbled overboard."

I gave White Hawk a sharp look, but I did not believe he would help them into the lake.

Marie also distrusted the men, for they would not follow her orders. During meals, instead of joining us, they carried their plates of ham and beans and biscuit to the opposite end of the deck, as if they were too good for us. I saw that they had no respect for Indians, for they were especially rude to White Hawk. They would have nothing to do with him. On so small a ship this took much effort.

Once I unexpectedly went belowdecks, and I found the two men closely examining the cargo of furs. Later, when I asked Marie if some of the cargo belonged to the two men, she answered, "Not one pelt. Those two don't know how to make an honest living."

After the first unpleasantness with the two men White Hawk and I paid them no attention. We had one day after another of blue sky and blue water. Along the shore there was nothing to see but sandy beaches and tall pines. The weather was so warm that even rain did not send White Hawk and me below. We put on old clothes and ran about barefooted helping Marie trim the sails. When the rain stopped we wrung the water from our hair and let the summer sun dry our clothes.

It was hot and stuffy below, so we often slept on deck. Every now and then we would catch sight of a campfire along the shore. Musing aloud, I asked White Hawk, "Who seems the most forlorn—our little boat in the middle of the lake or whoever is sitting alone along the shore with nothing around him but empty woods?"

"There's nothing forlorn about living alone in the woods, Mary," he answered. "Sometimes when I am in Detroit with houses and people all about me I long for the woods. Yet when I am alone in the woods I think of the pleasure of books and how they will give me the means to help my people."

"White Hawk, will you come back to the island to live?" I held my breath. I could not imagine the island without White Hawk.

"I don't know, Mary. I love the island as much as you do, but it might be more important for me to stay in Detroit and work with Pere Richard. I need to learn enough law to keep the Indians from being cheated out of their land."

While I was listening with an unhappy heart to White Hawk saying he might not return to Michilimackinac, the black sky above us suddenly came to life. Veils of restless color quivered and rippled over our heads. Even Marie became still and silent at the show. In a fit of friendliness I called belowdecks to Mr. Creaks and Mr. Soffle, "Come and see the northern lights!"

They stumbled up the ladder half asleep, looked suspiciously at us and then at the sky. After a minute they disappeared back down the ladder without a word. Disgusted, I said, "There is no money to be made from the spectacle. If they could have charged admission, no doubt they would have shown some interest."

White Hawk and I stayed up half the night and never tired of watching. White Hawk told me of an Indian legend he had once heard.

"The owls complained to one another in the night. 'Because Kitchimanittou has ordered us to go about in darkness, we see no colors. The other birds fly about among the flowers and see colors all day long.' The smaller owls said to the great gray owl, the largest of the owls, 'Go to Kitchimanittou. Tell him that we also wish to see color.' Kitchimanittou listened to the great gray owl. 'Go back to the other owls and tell them to look up the next time they fly about in the darkness.' That night when the owls looked up they saw that Kitchimanittou had spread the sky with all the colors of the flowers, reds and blues and purples and greens and yellows. And once again, the owls were content to fly about in the night."

With everyone else on the sloop asleep and the northern lights overhead, I felt like White Hawk and I were all alone in the world. I wished the night would never end.

With so little sleep I was slow to follow Marie's commands the next morning. As the wind shifted from northwest to southeast it was necessary to shift the sails. Marie called that she was putting the sloop about. I forgot to duck and as the heavy boom swung across the deck it caught me and sent me overboard. A moment later White Hawk dove after me. Since we were both good swimmers and the boom had done no more than given me a firm knock, there was no danger. Instead we carried on a water fight until Marie scolded us back onto the boat.

That afternoon we saw the mouth of the great Au Sable River emptying its waters into the lake. By using first the Au Sable and then the Manistee River as watery pathways, Indians were able to paddle all the way from Lake Michigan to Lake Huron. The next day we passed the Saginaw River. We knew we were only a few days from Detroit.

Then something very strange happened. Mr. Creaks and Mr. Soffle suddenly took a great interest in the land and in our progress. They were constantly inquiring about distances and questioning the landmarks on shore. Over and over they asked when we would reach the St. Clair River. White Hawk did not like their new mateyness. He whispered to me, "I have seen raccoons or foxes suddenly lose all their wariness and become tame as puppies. When that happens I look for some rabid sickness in the animal."

The next morning we were due to sail into the St. Clair River, which runs between our country and the shore of British Canada. Since we were heading toward the river the sloop was close to the American shore.

That night the two men hardly touched their dinner. Instead they kept searching along the beaches. We soon noticed three large campfires set next to one another on the shore. We thought little of it, for several tribes of the Ojibwa made their home in the area.

But at the sight of the fires, the two men hurried below. A moment later we were startled to see them scramble back up the ladder, Mr. Creaks with a pistol, Mr. Soffle with a knife. White Hawk and I were in the stern standing next to Pierre. Mr. Creaks stepped beside us, pointing the pistol at our heads. Mr. Soffle held the knife to Marie's throat. "Make for shore," he ordered. "We have some friends who will help you get rid of your cargo of furs."

I was too terrified to move. White Hawk looked at the pistol. I knew he wanted to grab it but was afraid a sudden movement might send a bullet into any one of us. I saw a quick glance exchanged between Pierre and Marie.

"Hurry up there," Mr. Creaks snarled.

Pierre put his hand on the tiller. Marie said, "Take that knife away if you want me to sail this boat."

Mr. Soffle pulled the knife a few inches away from Marie's throat and she reached for the rigging. The men had spent little time on deck. They had paid no attention to Pierre at the tiller or Marie's maneuvers with the sails. As soon as we saw Marie let go of the rope, Pierre, White Hawk, and I ducked. The heavy boom swung across the deck, sweeping Mr. Creaks and his pistol overboard.

White Hawk and Pierre lunged for Mr. Soffle, who was too stunned to move. With so much rope to hand they trussed him up like a roasting chicken. Mr. Creaks was thrashing about in the water, crying out that he could not swim. White Hawk shook his head and then, with a shrug, jumped overboard. In his terror Mr. Creaks nearly drowned White Hawk, who finally had to quiet him with a blow to the head, happily given.

Early the next morning we sailed into the St. Clair River. The entrance to the river was guarded by Fort Gratiot. We left Mr. Creaks and Mr. Soffle there, still closely wound around with rope. As the soldiers carried them off we heard them demand of the Bonnarts a refund of part of their passage, since they were not being taken all the way to Detroit!

Despite this misadventure, the rest of the trip was pleasant. From the St. Clair River the sloop, with only one dangerous turn at the southeast bend of the river, made its way among the grassy channel islands and into Lake St. Clair. Along the shore of the lake were the ribbon farms of French settlers.

"Each farm reaches back a mile from the shore," Marie told us. "Sometimes Pierre and I dream of settling down with an orchard of pears and apples like the ones our grandparents had in France. But we would surely spend all of our time staring at the water and no work would get done."

We were sailing along the Detroit River. Across the river was British Canada. Only a year before, our two countries had been at war. Now small ships and canoes and barges were free to cross the short distance from one country to the other. Looking out at the people standing on the Canadian shore I was relieved not to have to hate them.

As Detroit came into sight White Hawk pointed out the wooden houses and the flag flying over Fort Shelby. Pierre headed for a wharf made of logs and stone. I looked up at White Hawk and saw his eager smile.

"Now," he said, "I'll show you Detroit."

As happy as I was to have White Hawk as a guide, it was hard to take leave of Marie and Pierre. As soon as their cargo was carried off they would sail back to Michilimackinac. And I would travel farther and farther away from my island.

CHAPTER

6

DETROIT was my first city. While Michilimackinac had a huddle of small houses along its two streets, Detroit was a town of twenty-five hundred souls. Its houses were larger and newer than those on the island, for the whole city had burned to the ground only eleven years before. Much of what was built after the fire was destroyed once again, this time by the British and the Indians who fought alongside them.

Just as on Michilimackinac, Detroit had

soldiers and Indians and farmers and traders. But here the talk, often French, was brisker. People walked faster and smiled less.

White Hawk and I climbed into a little one-horse French cart, which carried us across the bridge on Market Street to St. Anne's Church. There Pere Richard, dressed in knee breeches and a long black coat reaching to his ankles, greeted White Hawk with enthusiasm and me in the warmest way.

I had heard much of Pere Richard—not only from White Hawk but from Papa as well. When the British conquered Detroit they demanded that the priest take an oath of allegiance to the king. He refused, saying, "I have taken one oath to support the Constitution of the United States and I cannot take another." He was carried away to Canada as a prisoner, but he was saved by the great Indian warrior Tecumseh, who had fought with the British. Tecumseh, knowing Pere Richard to be a friend of the Indians, made the British release him.

Pere Richard was a thin, sharp-featured man with a pair of glasses pushed up onto a wide fore-head. He had much to say to White Hawk, but once he saw how tired and worn I was from our trip he stopped himself. "Mary, my dear," he said with a strong French accent. "I have arranged for you to stay across the street from the church with the family of a Presbyterian minister, a friend of mine, the Reverend Monteith. It is a pity you must embark tomorrow on your journey east. There is much I could show you of my school. But let me just say a few words on my theories of instruction."

While I nearly fainted with fatigue and White Hawk shifted wearily from one foot to the other, Pere Richard went on, full of enthusiasm. "Always remember, children must be led to science and virtue by a flowery road. The hope of pleasure shall be the best allurement to study." I sank down on a nearby chair while White Hawk clasped a hand over his mouth to hide his grin.

"Forgive me, my children, I see you are near fainting with hunger. White Hawk, pray escort Mary across the street to the Monteiths' and then return and hear all of my news. The Reverend Monteith and myself are both to be professors of the new University of Michigania. And you shall be one of our first students. What do you say to that?"

On the way across the street White Hawk shook his head. "Pere Richard is always the teacher. He would teach day and night if he could. I hope he didn't weary you too much, Mary."

I was hanging on to White Hawk, trying not to dirty my skirts on the muddy streets. "I think his lessons are excellent ones," I said, laughing, "but they would come better after a good dinner."

The Monteiths were kindness itself, feeding me well and giving me the most comfortable bed to sleep upon. In the morning I said my farewells to Pere Richard, who could not keep from further instruction. "Remember, Mary, when you are a mother, the thorns of the most severe virtue are charming when they are conveniently twisted with the flowers of pleasure."

White Hawk and I managed to keep a straight face as we bid Pere Richard good-bye. I thanked him for all of his kindness and assured him I would not forget his lessons. White Hawk and I walked together to the wharf. We traveled slowly, for neither one of us was anxious to part. At last we arrived at the *Bluebird*, the schooner that was to carry me down the Detroit River and across Lake Erie to the city of Buffalo.

Hard as it had been to say farewell to the island, it was harder still to say good-bye to White Hawk. When I had left the island he had been with me. Now for the first time in my life I would be alone, and the distance ahead of me seemed endless. "What if I drown?" I said, trying to make my voice pitiful.

"There is no danger of that. You are like a cork in the water. And Mary, I will be here waiting to greet you when you return. Only promise you will not come back a proper English lady."

With a great effort I made myself smile. "I promise," I said. Only the thought of returning one day to White Hawk kept my spirits up.

We were on the lake nine days with only one storm and that not a bad one. Still, many of the passengers were affected. I shared a cabin with a woman and her two small children. The woman, a Mrs. Maupet, was laid very low by the rolling ship and I busied myself with caring for her little ones, Tom and Billy. They were lively and full of mischief. While I hung on to the shirt of one child, who was trying to climb over the gunwales, I was calling to the other, who was swinging from the mainyard. I tried to keep in mind Pere Richard's advice and twist my scoldings round with flowers of pleasure, but it was hard going. Sometimes there was nothing to do but take them by the ears.

When we reached Buffalo, with Mrs. Maupet better and both children still safely on board and not drowned, I thought I had done my duty. What with finding an inn in which to spend the night, and exploring the town, which like Detroit had seen much damage by the British, I gave them no further thought. I soon found an inn that looked out onto the Niagara River. I had heard much of the falls and listened for their thunder, but the distance was too great. I longed to see the famous sight, but I had a long journey ahead and a ship to meet. I could not risk a day.

Very early in the morning my trunk and I were put aboard a stagecoach. We stopped at a second inn to collect passengers, and to my great surprise, out came Tom and Billy and their mother. "What a pleasant surprise, Mary," Mrs. Maupet exclaimed. "Billy and Tom are so fond of you. You must help me to keep them occupied on our long journey to Albany."

"Mary! Mary!" the boys shouted. "We are traveling with you. Ain't you happy!"

The trip lasted two weeks, though it seemed much longer. It took us through towns whose strange names I had never heard before: Batavia, Canandaigua, Cozenovia, and Schenectady. Along the way were rich farms, blue lakes, gentle hills, and villages with fine homes.

There were also inns where the beds crawled with bugs and roads so muddy we had to get out of the coach and walk lest the wheels sink under our weight. In spite of the hardships I should have enjoyed all the new sights. But I did not have the chance. Mrs. Maupet did not know the word *obedience*. There was always one boy jumping on my lap and pounding on my bonnet and another one about to fall out of the window. It became my duty to keep the other passengers in the stage from murdering the boys in cold blood.

No matter how rough the tavern or inn where we spent our nights, the innkeeper always had a look of relief on his face as he waved us off, thankful the boys had left him no more than a few broken plates or a shattered lamp. When at last we reached Albany, Mrs. Maupet's destination, I breathed a sigh of relief. Yet to be truthful I owed much to the boys. In all my efforts to keep them alive I had had no time to feel lonesome.

The first leg of my journey was nearing an end. I had only to board a steamship and travel down the Hudson River to New York City, where Captain Frank Hodge and the *Comfort* were waiting. There were no steamships as yet on the Great Lakes, but steamships had been plying the Hudson River for ten years, ever since Mr. Fulton had invented them. This was the first time I had seen such a boat, with its two giant paddle wheels, one on each side of the boat. It was a frightening sight, for smoke and sparks poured out of its tall chimney. Though it carried sails the boat did not have to depend on them. Whatever the direction of the wind we still moved along at the incredible speed of fifteen miles an hour! Still, I much preferred the silent wings of the sailboat to the racketty noise of the steamboat's machinery and paddles.

But despite the noise, the trip down the Hudson could not have been more pleasant. South of Albany there were prosperous farms spread over gentle hills. Soon the Catskill Mountains, lavender and blue and gold, loomed in the distance. The mouths of the rivers that flowed into the Hudson were marked by flour or lumber mills. The mill wheels were turned by the rivers as they splashed into the great Hudson. There were mansions such as I had never imagined with wide porches and lawns stretching down to the riverbank. When darkness fell, candles and lanterns blinked over the land like so many fireflies.

As we neared New York we passed the granite boulders of West Point, and five hundred feet above it, Fort Putnam. In the misty September twilight it was not hard to imagine General Washington commanding his troops atop the rocky pile. I could almost see the great iron chain whose links once stretched across the Hudson to keep the British from sailing up the river.

We steamed into New York City early on a Saturday morning. After the long lazy voyage down the Hudson, the tumble of buildings along the Battery and the hurry and bustle of the hundreds of boats in the city's harbor was like a thunderclap. I was amazed to see buildings three and four stories high, with one building leaning against another so that the people nested together like hens in a coop.

As the men were making ready to lower the gangplank I asked one of them if he could pick out the *Comfort* from all the ships in the harbor.

"The *Comfort*, is it, little lady? Why, we all know it. It's not every day we get a British ship of such size and importance. A year ago our *Constitution* would have welcomed the chance to take it on. There it is, in all its glory." He pointed to a huge three-story ship anchored at the harbor's entrance. Its sails were furled, but its three great masts reached to the clouds. The ship was all black and gold, with the Union Jack fluttering at its bow.

I had expected a schooner like the one I had taken on Lake Erie, only a bit larger. I had not imagined anything like the *Comfort*, and I had no idea what would be expected of me on such a fine ship. But fainthearted as the grandeur of the ship made me, I could not delay. My instructions were to go aboard as soon as I reached the city, and I was only a day from the sailing date.

CHAPTER

7

AS I DISEMBARKED, a barge was pointed out to me not far from our berth. "That'll belong to the *Comfort*," I was told. "Looks like they're just getting ready to cast off."

I left my trunk and hurried to where the barge was tied up. Timidly I approached one of the crew. Like all the sailors on the barge he was dressed in loose-fitting trousers and a striped sweater with a kerchief tied about his neck. He wore slippers with bows and a shiny black hat with a dangling ribbon embroidered with the word *Comfort*. He was an older man, with a tanned, wrinkled face and a pleasant smile. What caught my attention most was his hair, which was plaited and hung nearly to his waist.

Taking a deep breath, I said, "Good morning. I'm Mary O'Shea and I believe Captain Hodge is expecting me."

"Heavens, yes, mam. We've been looking for you these last three days. The captain thought he might have to sail without you. Rachert's my name. Let me get your trunk and then I'll help you aboard. As soon as Mr. Lindsay comes we'll head for the ship."

As the trunk was being carried on, a young man in white trousers, a blue jacket with a white patch on the collar, and a top hat hurried toward the barge. He looked to be about Jacques's age. He had the fair complexion that never darkens but only burns in the sun, and yellow curls reaching to his neck. He appeared in a great hurry. As he jumped onto the barge he made some attempt to apologize. The men made no comment, for in spite of his youth he was clearly in charge of them. Mr. Rachert did urge the crew to "pull hard" on the oars.

With a startled look Mr. Lindsay suddenly

discovered me among the crew. "You must be Miss O'Shea." He looked relieved. "Captain Hodge will be pleased to see you, mam. Let's hope he'll be too occupied with getting you settled to notice we're late. I'm James Lindsay, at your service." As a bit of water from the oars dropped onto my dress, Mr. Lindsay called out, "Row dry there, Rachert."

He seemed young to be giving such experienced men orders. I wondered if he was trying to impress me with his importance. To assure him that it was not necessary, I replied in a firm voice, "I don't mind a little water in the least."

As we approached the frigate it grew larger and larger. I saw no way at all of getting up her side. There was a rough rope netting, but it stretched three stories high and I knew I couldn't climb it in skirts and petticoats. But I needn't have worried. Mr. Lindsay hailed the ship and called out, "Ahoy there, send down a bosun's chair." At that, a kind of wooden swing was lowered and I was fastened into it and drawn up on deck while Mr. Lindsay and the other crew scrambled up the rope ladder.

I landed directly in front of a large man in the most elegant uniform I had ever seen. He wore blue breeches and a blue jacket trimmed all over with gold, and a gold epaulette on each shoulder. On his head was a tricornered hat decorated with gold braid. He fair shone with gold. He had dark hair and dark eyes with thick eyebrows, and a thin mouth that was now drawn into a smile though nothing in his manner suggested pleasure.

"How do you do, mam," he said. "We have been looking for you these last days. I am Captain Hodge and I am delighted to wait upon you. I hope we will give you a pleasant journey."

I was aware that I was probably looked upon as a nuisance aboard, so I was anxious to please. "How do you do, sir. It is so good of you to carry me on your ship. I'll try to give you no trouble. In return for your kindness I hope I can be of some use. I know how to shift sails and I'm not afraid of heights." I looked doubtfully at the tall masts.

There was a dreadful silence and I was aware of the crew looking from me to the captain. Behind the captain Mr. Lindsay was fighting a smile. So he did not take himself so seriously after all. The captain looked more stern than seemed possible and said in the coldest voice, "Mam, with a crew of four hundred men I daresay we can manage without having to call upon you." He swung around and caught Mr. Lindsay's smile. "Mr. Lindsay, there, wipe that smirk from your face and explain why the barge was a half hour past its appointed time. I suppose you were waiting for Miss O'Shea?"

"It was all my fault, sir," replied Mr. Lindsay. "I was late getting to the barge and I most sincerely regret it." It would have been easy for Mr. Lindsay to agree with the captain and blame the lateness on me. I thought well of him for not doing so.

"Well, sir," the captain responded. "Let us see you at the topgallant crosstrees."

The young man walked briskly to the tallest of the three masts. He climbed up and up until I had to bend my neck to see him at all. When he was nearly at the top he settled down on the pole from which the highest sail hung. And there he stayed.

The captain turned to me. "Miss O'Shea, Mr. Rachert will take you below. We have set aside a small cabin for you and I hope you will be comfortable. Now, if you will excuse me, I seem to have some weather to deal with."

As I followed Mr. Rachert I looked over my shoulder and saw on the far horizon a cloud as dark as the look on the captain's face when he sent Mr. Lindsay to the top of the mast. "Will Mr. Lindsay be allowed to come down if it rains?" I asked Mr. Rachert. I could not keep from looking at the young man perched at a dizzying height above the deck.

"Never worry about him, mam. He's happy as a lark up there. He'll have his pencil and paper out by now, making one of his pictures. If the lightning gets bad the captain will call him down. Mr. Lindsay and the other midshipmen just about live up there. Down this ladder, mam. Watch how you go, one hand for yourself, the other for the ship."

My cabin, though tiny, was a model of comfort. A hammock swung from the walls. There was a chair and a small table with a washbasin and pitcher. A lantern cast a yellow glow, lighting even the dark corners. I was sure I would be happy there in the weeks ahead. Still, I wished I had made a better start with Captain Hodge.

When I had unpacked what was needed from my trunk, I poked my head up the hatchway to find that the rain was indeed coming down in great sheets. I stretched my neck to look up at the rigging, and there was a very wet Mr. Lindsay. He had fastened himself onto the mast with his belt. I went back to my cabin angry with the captain for his cruelty.

Mr. Rachert brought dinner to me that evening on a tray. "Am I not to eat with the others, Mr. Rachert?"

"Well, I don't see it, miss. The crew would be out of the question, and it wouldn't be suitable for you to dine in the wardroom with the officers. The captain dines alone, though he will have you to dinner one day, I'm sure."

"What about the midshipmen?" Since they were only young men in training to be officers, I thought it might be suitable for me to join them. To tell the truth, I was thinking of Mr. Lindsay.

"Oh, miss, you'd as soon sit down to dine in a cage of monkeys."

When breakfast came on a tray as well, I began to think it would be a lonely voyage. I saw two eggs on my dish and asked Mr. Rachert where they had come from.

"Oh, we carry hens, pigs, sheep, and goats for milk."

"It sounds like the ark." I was cheered to learn the ship was not so different from a farm. "Where are they kept?"

"Down in the hold, miss, but in fine weather we bring them up for a bit of air. You'll see them on deck today."

"Then the rain has stopped?"

"The sky is as blue as you could wish."

"Would I be allowed on deck?"

"You would be very welcome, I'm sure. Only, of course, not on the windward side of the quarterdeck, as that is reserved for the captain. The captain has hoisted the blue peter, the flag that says the ship is ready to sail. If you go right up you'll be in time to see the ship catch the tide."

I put on my bonnet and threw a shawl about my shoulders. On deck I found four hundred men scurrying about setting the sails and weighing anchor. They were clambering up and down all three masts and hanging over the bowsprit as well. I thought of how White Hawk and I had taken pleasure in helping the Bonnarts with the sailing of their sloop. On the *Comfort* I was useless. But my unhappiness disappeared as I watched one sail after another unfurled until I thought the ship would fly right off the water. I could not help exclaiming aloud.

Someone said, "It is a glorious sight."

It was Mr. Lindsay. I saw that his arm was in a sling.

Alarmed, I asked, "What happened?"

He looked puzzled. "Oh, you mean my arm.

It's nothing. Just a sprain. Coming down in the rain I found the shroud a bit slippery."

"The shroud?"

"The rope I came down."

"It was terrible for the captain to leave you up there."

"Not at all. A less kindly captain would have had me flogged for my lateness. Time is everything on a ship, you know. Anyhow, it's only my left hand. My working and drawing hand is fine."

"Yes, Mr. Rachert said you sketched. Are you an artist?"

"Not in the least. I am only a beginner, but it's why I went to sea. I have a great desire to draw ships, not sail them, but my family thinks poorly of artists and well of sailors. I'll tell you a secret. It's why I was late for the barge yesterday. You Americans have an artist, Washington Allston, who paints fine pictures of ships. His paintings were on display yesterday in New York and I knew it would be the only chance I had to see them. Now I must look lively or the captain will have me mastheaded again."

A small procession of animals appeared on the forward deck. There were several cages of hens, two goats, four pigs, and five sheep. I hurried over to the animals, deeply lonesome for Belle and our pigs. "Are you taking them to England?" I asked one of the crew.

"Oh, no, miss," replied the man, who introduced himself as Mr. Craig. "The captain and the officers eat the eggs and a hen or two, and over the course of the voyage the pigs and sheep. The goats we keep for the milk."

"The crew and midshipmen don't have any meat?"

"We have our salt pork and our salt horse and biscuit, miss."

"You have horsemeat?" I thought of how the British soldiers on our island had been so desperate for food during the war they had butchered their horses.

"That's only a manner of speaking. Salt horse is salted beef. Now, if you'll pardon me, I'll just commence the milking—though I'd as soon see a pirate come after me with his cutlass and pistol."

I watched as he pulled a stool next to the goat and began to milk. He was rough and unskilled and the goat knew it. In a moment the goat had a piece of his shirt between her teeth and the next moment she was skittering across the deck.

"There, you see," Mr. Craig said in disgust.

"And the cook waiting for the milk for the captain's pudding." He captured the goat and this time tied her up.

"Let me try," I offered. "Back home I milked our cow, Belle."

He gave a quick look about, and seeing no one watching us, gave up his stool with great relief. I petted the goat and spoke gently to her. When I started to milk her, she stayed put. In no time the pail was full.

But when I looked up, expecting praise for my success, I saw Mr. Craig standing so stiffly at attention I thought he might crack. Staring down at me was Captain Hodge. I stumbled to my feet, nearly upsetting the pail.

"I see, Miss O'Shea, you still wish to be helpful."

I began to explain, but not wanting to mention Mr. Craig's troubles in front of his captain, I soon stumbled.

"With whatever small influence I have on the ship, mam, I must once again beg you to leave the tasks to its crew." With that he turned on his heel and marched away.

"Oh, Mr. Craig," I apologized. "I hope I have not got you into trouble."

"No, miss. And next time I go to milk the

goat I'll remember to speak as sweetly to her as you did."

Left to myself I explored the ship. There were numerous decks, ladders, and hatches. Everything had its place. The hammocks the crew slept in each night were rolled up and placed neatly away during the day. All ropes were carefully coiled. Decks shone from their morning polishing. Stored belowdecks in the hold was all the food and water needed for our long voyage.

Just as there was a place for everything, there was a time for everything as well. Bells sounded on the half hour to tell the watches or the times for meals. On Sundays an awning was put up on the deck. A kind of church service was held and all the crew assembled dressed in their best. The captain read from the Book of Common Prayer or the Articles of War, depending on his mood. The Articles of War were very frightening in their listing of the terrible punishments given for disobedience.

On Thursdays misbehavior was noted. If a crew member was named for waywardness, his punishment was read out. The captain asked if anyone had something good to say for the man. At that, an officer might speak up and proclaim the man a steady and sober worker and the punishment would be lessened.

On one terrible occasion when a man had stolen and no one spoke up for him, I was sent below while he was flogged. Later when I came back on deck I saw the crew scrubbing away at bloodstains. I thought poorly of Captain Hodge for this and wondered at the men who had no word of criticism for their captain. "You know the rules when you sign on, miss," Mr. Rachert said. "Our captain is as fair a man as you could wish for."

On Wednesday the crew scrubbed and mended their clothes. Many of them were skilled with needles and thimbles. The greatest fun on that day was to see the men wash their long hair and then take turns plaiting it into pigtails with the help of a friend. In the evenings the crew would bring hornpipes and fiddles onto the deck and the men would dance and sing.

But my greatest pleasure of all was in watching the crew hoist the sails. On days when the wind was in just the right quarter the men would climb the rigging and shake out all the sails. I longed to climb one of the masts. Mr. Lindsay said on a clear day you could see for ten miles and more from the main-topgallant yard. He was often up there with the rest of the midshipmen, hoisting the sails, taking in or shaking out the reefs that were tucks in the sails. At times they would do what they called skylarking—swinging about in the rigging in the same way White Hawk and Jacques and I used to climb the great pine trees on the island so that we might look out at the lake.

As the days passed I grew to dread the loneliness of having meals in my solitary cabin. When the captain invited me to dine with him one evening, I accepted with pleasure. That afternoon I happened into the galley. It was a place I often visited, for I admired the rows of copper pots so shiny you could see your face in them. I was astounded at the size of the huge barrels that held the cook's supplies—flour and sugar and ship's biscuits. The cook, Mr. Bingham, was a short, fat man wrapped in a dirty towel. He was usually friendly but this day he was cross. "You're causing me any amount of trouble today, miss."

"What do you mean, Mr. Bingham?"

"You dine with the captain this evening and he's called for a French sauce with the fish. I know nothing of French sauces. What can the captain be thinking of? Two years ago he was sending cannonballs across the bows of the French, now he asks for one of their sauces. It's as good as a surrender."

"What is the name of the sauce?"

"Betcha ma or some such."

"*Béchamel*, Mr. Bingham. I've made it many times. My mother was French, and when she died she left me and my sister her recipes. Let me help."

He looked doubtful, but at last he stood aside. In no time I had melted the butter, slowly worked in the flour, pounding out the lumps, added the milk, and stirred it to a fine silkiness. It was Papa's favorite sauce. "It must cook slowly now for a half hour and you must never cease stirring it," I cautioned him.

Mr. Bingham stared gratefully into the pot and then at me. "Well, miss, you must have some Frenchified blood in you. But I don't hold it against you."

I was aware of the honor of eating with the captain and brought out my best dress and my ermine pelisse. It was with something like terror that I made my way across the sacred quarter-deck, where only the captain walked, and from there to his quarters. He was at his door to greet me, looking elegant in white silken breeches and silk stockings and a coat bright with gold lace. "Welcome, mam. I assure you this is a pleasure."

He led me into a suite of rooms that took my breath away. I had seen the little cubbyholes in which the officers bunked and I thought of my own tiny cabin with no window. Here before me was a great room with a sweep of windows looking out at the sea. The dining table was set with a snowy cloth and a spread of silver. I had never dined in such splendor.

"Oh, sir . . ." I began. But I could say nothing more, for I was truly speechless.

"You do me an honor, mam, for captains must keep apart from their crew. It is a lonely life."

"Sir, why must you keep apart?"

"Surely you have heard that familiarity breeds contempt." How then, I wondered, had we all lived together so happily on our island?

The captain continued, "And then the officers and midshipmen who are invited to dine from time to time are aware I am their captain, and the conversation is so checked by their reserve I might as well be by myself. I hope you will be more forthcoming."

With this encouragement I chattered on, for I am not one to lack for words. In his turn he told me of the trip on which he carried the British troops and Angelique back to England after the end of the war. "Your sister was most ladylike. Never gave me a moment's trouble."

I told him of life on our island. He was so pleasant, I dared ask, "I don't suppose, sir, I might try climbing one of the masts. I do so long to sit up there and look out at the ocean."

Captain Hodge frowned. "Completely unsuitable, mam. We could not have it." And then more kindly, "It's not as easy as it looks, you know."

Before I could tell him of the many trees I had climbed, the dinner commenced. It began with a lobster soup. "Fished them out on Canada's grand banks," the captain said of the lobsters, "and kept them alive just for such soup."

The first course was removed and the fish course brought in, swimming in its sauce. I was relieved to see Mr. Bingham had not allowed it to burn. After the fish we had mutton chops and then a delicious pudding.

Captain Hodge had much to say that was interesting. He had seen action against Capt. Oliver Perry on Lake Huron and spoke well of our navy though he had fought against it. He even knew where Michilimackinac was. "I grew up on an island myself, mam. The Isle of Wight. As a boy I watched the great ships sail from Portsmouth past my home, out of the channel and across the seven seas. I never considered a life other than that of a sailor. I signed on to my first ship when I was ten years old. I only fear that with the war against America over and Napoleon locked away my sailing days may be finished."

"Why should that be?"

"Two thirds of the ships like this one will be taken off the sea. There are hundreds of officers like myself competing for commands of the few ships that will remain. And I am not high on the list."

"Mayn't you go back to your island and have a small sloop to sail about in?" I was thinking of how I longed for my own island.

"It would not be quite like this."

I looked about the great windowed cabin with its view of the sea, at the fine furniture, the silver upon the table, and the servants standing behind each of our chairs, and I had to agree that a small sloop would not serve a man accustomed to so noble a ship. To cheer him I complimented him again on the fine dinner.

"Yes, the cook did well. Jarvas," he said to

one of the servants, "run down to the galley and ask the cook to come up."

Mr. Bingham arrived looking worried. He was quickly cheered by the captain's congratulations.

"The béchamel sauce was especially tasty," said the captain. "I believe you told me you had never made it before."

"Oh, sir, if I may say so, the credit for that bit must go to the young lady here. It was she who fixed up the sauce."

The captain stared at me. "You were in the galley cooking today?" he asked in a sort of hoarse voice.

"Yes, sir." Seeing the expression on his face I hastily added, "Just giving the sauce a stir."

"Thank you, Bingham, you may go." He turned to me. "I was indeed foolish, mam, to think a mere veteran of thirty years in His Majesty's service, including many battles and any number of wounds, might command my vessel without the ample help of a young woman. Perhaps I should apply to the Admiral of the Fleet to give you a commission for your own ship."

My face was scarlet with embarrassment. It seemed a good time to leave, but as I turned to go he said, "Still, for such a sauce I must forgive you."

As I turned back and looked up into his face I saw he was fighting back a grin. I thanked him heartily for his hospitality. "When I get my commission, sir," I said, "I hope I may be as fine a captain as you are." I hurried from the cabin and was still on the quarterdeck when I heard Captain Hodge's laughter.

CHAPTER

8

MOST OF MY TIME was spent on the deck looking out at the great stretch of ocean, half wishing I was home and half wishing I was in London. The crew were very kind to me. They were always willing to answer my endless questions about the shifting of sails and the strange birds that flew over the ship and the fish that swam beside it. There was the impressive spectacle of gunnery practice, when the great guns were rolled out and fired. The practice caused a terrible noise and smoke so thick you could not see from one side of the deck to the other. Although Great Britain had no enemy at present, the crew said Napoleon had escaped once and might do so again. I thought they almost hoped he would, for they never tired of boasting of the battles they had fought against the French.

One day Mr. Lindsay brought me on deck to see a whale. A fearsome creature, it rolled along like a floating island.

"It is like the Leviathan of the scriptures," I said, thinking of the book of Job. "'It makes the deep boil like a pot.'" And indeed, just at that moment a great spout rushed forth from the whale, startling us both into laughter.

Mr. Lindsay and I became friends. He told me of his longing to be an artist and his father's opposition to his dreams. He even let me look through his sketchbook. It was wonderful to see how he had captured not only the ship's appearance but the look of the crew in their daily tasks. And in one frightening picture a sketch of the man being lashed. "How could you draw such a terrible thing?" I asked.

"Punishment is a part of life on board the ship," Mr. Lindsay said. "I refuse to do only pretty things. I mean to show all of life. At home I have sketchbooks filled with drawings I have made of some of the ugliest parts of London."

It surprised me that someone should take time to copy out ugly things, but I could not help but admire Mr. Lindsay's talent. In my turn I told Mr. Lindsay of life on my island. I told him of Jacques and Little Cloud and how it broke my heart that they would have the farm. He never tired of hearing stories of the Indians and how they dressed and lived. "One day, Miss O'Shea," he said, "I'll come to your island and paint it."

It was Mr. Lindsay who invited me to dine with the midshipmen. "Peters has been fishing off the side and caught some haddock. Erickson has some of his mother's gooseberry jam tucked away, and the cook says he can turn it into a respectable boiled pudding." Eagerly, I accepted.

I wore no ermine pelisse when I went to the midshipmen's berth. I had been warned by Mr. Lindsay. "It will be like eating in a pig's pen. But I'll see they are all on their best behavior."

And so they were. There were fifteen of them, some as young as eleven or twelve, most in their teens and some, like Mr. Lindsay, nearing twenty. Their quarters were cramped and dank, well down in the ship and with no window, but the floor and table had been well scrubbed. The midshipmen, quite neat in clean shirts and blue brass-buttoned jackets, stood at attention to receive me. I was seated with great courtesy.

At first they all just looked at me and I began to think there was something very wrong with my appearance, but a midshipman named Becker solved the problem for me.

"You must forgive these louts for staring. We haven't had a meal with a girl for a year, mam, and we hardly know what to say."

I was greatly relieved at his honesty and hastened to reassure them. "You must treat me as you would your sisters," I laughed. "I have a lively brother and I'm not at all afraid of boys." At that they seemed to relax.

There was a loud rapping on the table with spoons and stamping of feet to call in the cook— not Mr. Bingham, but a more scruffy man I had seen lurking in the corners of the galley. He set a plate of fish on the table. One of the midshipmen started to lunge toward it, but the boy beside him stabbed him none too gently with his fork, crying out, "Have you no manners, Corson? Ladies first."

There was no silver service to pass as there

had been in the captain's quarters. Instead the boy nearest the fish speared a piece and deposited it on my plate. The fish was tasty and I told them so.

"You must eat very well," I said.

At that there was great laughter. "Oh, miss," Mr. Corson said, "it's salt pork if we're lucky and at the end of a long voyage rats are a treat."

"Rats!" I could hardly believe him.

"Of course we don't call them rats. We refer to them with great delicacy as millers."

"Millers? Do you mean men who work in the flour mills?"

"Yes, the rats crawl about in the flour barrels and get all chalky, like little white ghosts. But skinned and dressed out they are quite tasty—rather like squirrel."

"When we run out of rats," Mr. Corson said, "we get our meat ration from biscuit."

"But biscuits aren't meat, surely?"

Mr. Corson grinned. "It ain't the biscuit but what lives in the biscuit," he said. "Cockroaches, maggots, and weevils."

At this, Becker began throwing biscuits at Corson. "There's your meat ration, Corson. Have you no manners to talk like that over dinner?"

Mr. Corson returned biscuit for biscuit and

there commenced a general dispersal of everything on the table. Since I have always had a rather good throwing arm, I soon joined in, finding the biscuits much like the stones upon the beaches of Michilimackinac.

Things quieted a bit when the gooseberry pudding was brought in, and for a moment mouths were too full for much talk. During the silence I said, "How I envy all of you getting to climb to the top of the masts. I'd give anything to do that."

"You'd fall on your head," Mr. Becker said.

"No, I wouldn't," I protested. "I've climbed to the top of pine trees nearly as tall."

"Why shouldn't she do it if she wishes?" Mr. Lindsay cried out. "We could dress her up like us! Braid her hair."

"Lindsay, you could give her some of your clothes," Becker said. "They're disgustingly clean."

Mr. Lindsay grinned. "We'll do it this afternoon. The captain is in his cabin every Wednesday going over the accounts with the purser."

After that everything happened quickly. I took Mr. Lindsay's clothes to my cabin and changed into them, braided my hair into a long pigtail, and pulled a hat well down over my head. Mr. Lindsay and Mr. Corson were waiting for me on deck. I had seen the crew climb up and down the rigging as easily as monkeys, but now that it was my turn I hesitated, for in truth none of the trees I had climbed were nearly as tall. And the masts had no branches.

Seeing me hesitate, Mr. Lindsay said, "You needn't do this, you know."

By then I could not turn back. I would have shamed myself in front of all the midshipmen, especially Mr. Lindsay. Tentatively I put a foot on the ratlines, which are a sort of rope ladder.

"Hang on to the shrouds as you climb, and whatever you do, don't look down," Mr. Lindsay said. "I'll be right behind you."

Up I went. Up and up and up. Halfway up there was a kind of platform, and if I had been in possession of my senses I would have stopped there. But I was aware of Mr. Lindsay behind me and I wanted to show him I was not afraid. So I kept going. Up and up and up. Mr. Lindsay cheered me on. Finally I reached the pole from which hung the very top sail of the mainmast.

I clung to the pole for dear life and looked out at the ocean. I was above the birds and sure that if I reached up I could touch the clouds. There was ocean as far as I could see, a great spread of it like a bolt of green cloth thrown out. "Oh!" I whispered, my fear gone for a moment. "It's more wonderful than I imagined."

Mr. Lindsay climbed out on the other side of the pole.

"There is nothing like it," he said. "No matter how I mix my paints I cannot capture the hue. It is one color one minute and another the next. But we must go down now. We don't want the crew to recognize you."

Before he could warn me again I looked down and knew at once all was lost. The deck glimpsed between the sails looked a million miles away; the men on the deck no more than ants. I was frozen in fear and could not move. I shook my head, unable to find words.

"Come now," Mr. Lindsay said kindly. "Look upward and just put one foot down and then another. I'll be right beneath you guiding your feet."

"I can't," I said, my voice no more than a whisper.

"There is nothing to it. I've done it a thousand times."

"I can't," I squeaked.

His voice was becoming impatient. "The

crew is beginning to wonder what we are doing up here. You must come down."

I would have given anything to be able to move my foot an inch, but I could not. No amount of assurance or entreaty helped. When Mr. Lindsay tried to move me, I screamed, and he had to stop at once. "Be quiet!" he warned. "They will hear you on deck."

It seemed hours passed, though I believe it was just minutes. Mr. Lindsay's voice was half angry and half desperate. Below us on the deck a knot of men was looking up and then the knot drew apart. I heard a terrible voice like thunder rising from the deck.

"Mr. Lindsay, come down at once, ye hear me!"

Mr. Lindsay's voice trembled. "The captain!" He reached for the nearest rope and slid down to the deck. I was left alone.

The next thing I knew the captain was beside me, panting a little from the climb, a furious look on his face. "You are worse than a stubborn kitten stuck in a tree," he said. With that he took hold of me and, in spite of my screams, slung me over his shoulder and started down. When I felt the deck beneath my feet I ran to my cabin, my cheeks wet with tears, believing myself thoroughly disgraced.

I kept to my cabin the rest of the day. When Mr. Rachert brought my dinner tray he said, "Well, miss, you are the talk of the ship. We all admired the way you got to the top. I wouldn't want to be James Lindsay, though. He's apt to have a bad time of it tomorrow morning when the punishment is given out."

That night I had not only my own foolishness to keep me awake but the trouble I had made for James Lindsay.

In the morning I longed to remain in my cabin. But when, as usual on Thursdays, "All hands to witness punishment" was piped, I made myself go up onto the deck. I had shown enough cowardice the day before. As I took my place I felt all eyes on me, especially the captain's. He read the terrible Articles of War. It seemed the death sentence was required for every other article. If not the death sentence, then "such other punishment as the nature and degree of the offence shall deserve."

As he had read out Article Two, condemning "scandalous actions in derogation of God's honor, and corruption of good manners," he stared right at Mr. Lindsay.

There was not a sound to be heard on deck.

Captain Hodge asked his master-at-arms to name any member of the crew guilty of disobeying the articles. The master-at-arms said, "Mr. Lindsay, sir, guilty of Article Two."

Captain Hodge, looking very severe, said, "Mr. Lindsay, have you anything to say for yourself?"

"Only that I regret my actions, sir."

Captain Hodge turned to the officers. "Do you have anything to say in Mr. Lindsay's behalf?"

I could not stop myself. I could not be responsible for having Mr. Lindsay hanged or flogged. Before anyone could speak, I stepped forward. "It is not Mr. Lindsay's fault, sir," I blurted out. "I said that I wished to climb the mast. It was all my doing."

At my words I could hear a gasp go around the ship like a gale. Mr. Lindsay got very red. The captain glared at me. Finally he said, "Double watches for the remainder of the trip, Mr. Lindsay."

I breathed a great sigh of relief and tried to catch Mr. Lindsay's eye. But he would not look at me. He only looked very furious.

That night, as Mr. Rachert brought in my tray, he gave me a thoughtful look. "Well, miss, you're the talk of the ship once more."

"I couldn't keep still. A word had to be said for Mr. Lindsay."

"That was for the officers to do. I daresay they would have spoken up. Mr. Lindsay is well liked, though I doubt he'll make lieutenant now."

My heart sank as I thought of the mischief I had done. "But what if the captain had ordered him hanged or flogged?"

"No danger of having him hanged. Captain wouldn't waste rope on the likes of him. As to flogging, I believe Mr. Lindsay had much rather had a hundred strokes than have a young woman speak out for him in front of the crew."

With that he left me. I saw what I had done. With my foolish speaking out I had embarrassed Mr. Lindsay in front of the whole ship. I was sure he would hate me forever, but not as much as I hated myself.

In my misery I crept below to be with the animals, for I knew they would not pass judgment on me. The pens were not cleaned well and the smell was strong. The sheep and most of the hens were eaten, but the goats and one of the pigs were still there. The pig appeared to be ill. He was thin and weak with a runny nose and eyes and a wicked cough. I went to the cook. "Mr. Bingham, the pig has hog flu. You had better tell the captain the pig ought to be butchered, sooner rather than later, or he will die on you. Also, the captain should know the animals' pens are in a sorry state."

That evening there was a pork chop on my plate. Mr. Rachert announced, "Captain's compliments, miss. He says to tell you he is pleased you still have the ship well in hand."

I smiled but I had no heart for the chop. I could not sleep, and though I heard all through the night the usual cry of "All's well," it was not well with me. Although I had passed him on deck several times that day, Mr. Lindsay would not look my way.

Two days later, before it was swallowed in a veil of fog, we sighted Land's End, the tip of England. The next day, with a strong southwest wind to hurry us, we sailed past Captain Hodge's Isle of Wight and into Portsmouth. Our voyage was over.

CHAPTER
9

*B*EFORE I WAS let down onto the barge that would carry me and my trunk to shore, I thanked Captain Hodge for all he had done to make my voyage a comfortable one. "I hope I have not been too mettlesome, sir."

"Mettlesome, mam? No, indeed. We have never had so merry a sailing, nor has the ship ever been so well managed. You must be sure to warn me—I mean to say, you must be sure to *tell* me—when you plan to make a return passage."

We parted friends and I believed that once on shore, where he no longer had to command, Captain Hodge would be a kindly man.

As the barge carried me away from the *Comfort* I saw Mr. Lindsay on deck looking down at us. I gave a timid wave of my hand but he looked away.

In a few minutes the barge landed and I stepped out to find Angelique's arms about me.

"Oh, Mary!" she cried. "I am so happy to see you!" We could not cease hanging on to one another.

"How did you know when the *Comfort* would be here?"

"In London we know where all the ships are. The fishing sloops and other small boats keep a lookout and pass the news on. I have been here awaiting your arrival. Now we must hurry. The chaise is ready to leave. It's a two-day journey to London and we can talk all the way. I have so much I want to tell you, and you must tell me every single thing that has happened since I left the island."

"Don't we have to wait for the other passengers?" I asked, for the handsome carriage was empty.

"The carriage belongs to Daniel's family.

They kindly lent it to me for our journey. Daniel and I live with the Cunninghams, you know. Their house is a large one." She sighed a small sigh. "Though, large as it is, it is sometimes too small for two families."

As she hurried me to the carriage I could not take my eyes from Angelique. From the loopy twists and coils of her curls to her silk dress, which was all tucks and ruffles, she was the picture of elegance. I could not help asking, "Where do your toes go in those pointed boots? They must be all piled up on one another."

Angelique settled us into the chaise. "Do you remember when Daniel saw me with dirty bare feet? That was all your doing, Mary. Daniel is grateful to you, for he tells me it showed him that I lacked the affectation of so many of the girls he had known in England. It gave him the courage to propose to me. Daniel is anxious to see you, Mary."

"Are you happy you married him, Angelique?"

"Yes, of course. I love him very much, and his family is so kind to me. His father is good-natured and his mother is teaching me to be a lady."

"What do you mean, teaching you? You were

a lady to begin with. Not like me."

"Mrs. Cunningham's standards are very high, Mary. She goes about in the best society. She is very strict in her expectations. One thing I must warn you of. I have not told her Jacques's wife is an Indian."

"Why ever not!"

"On the island no one thinks anything of it, but I'm afraid Mrs. Cunningham would not understand it."

"I daresay Little Cloud is more of a lady than any women of Mrs. Cunningham's acquaintance." I began to tell Angelique of Jacques's marriage and how clever Little Cloud was. I told her, too, of my disappointment in Jacques's having the farm. "It's selfish of me, but I can't help it."

"If the farm is not to be yours, why should you go back to work digging about in the dirt and slopping pigs?" Angelique asked. "I am sure I can find you a very suitable husband right here. Then we would always be together."

"You are just like Mrs. West," I chided her. "She would have me married to a London man as well. What would I do if I did not return to Michilimackinac and the dirt and the pigs?"

After that, no more was said about finding me

a husband. Instead we talked as fast as we could, telling one another tales of the island and of London. We talked on the journey and we talked half the night in the inn and we talked our way into London. Still we hadn't finished.

The sight of London finally silenced me. I knew it to be the largest city in the world, with over a million souls, but I was unprepared for the crowded streets, teeming with people. Angelique had to hold on to my skirts to keep me from falling out of the carriage window, for I could not stop looking.

My amazement at the city was nothing compared to my astonishment at the home of the Cunninghams. The carriage turned onto a square with a statue of King George III on a horse and many fine trees, the like of which I had never seen.

"Plane trees," Angelique told me. "They are hardy, and don't mind living in the city with its fog and smoke. The Cunninghams' house is over there across Berkeley Square."

I saw a redbrick home of four stories. The entrance was through a wrought-iron archway, crowned on its top by a large wrought-iron lantern. A liveried footman opened the door to the house. Angelique sailed through the door and I crept along behind her, terrified of tripping or otherwise disgracing myself. A tall, handsome woman in a lavender silk dress and lace cap greeted us.

"This is my sister, Mary, mam," Angelique said.

"You are very welcome, Mary. I am Mrs. Cunningham. We have looked forward to your visit with great pleasure. We hope you will be happy with us."

The words were kindness itself, but all the while they were spoken I noticed Mrs. Cunningham was taking in my clothes. Until now I had thought them well enough, but under her disapproving eyes they became rags and tatters. When her eyes shifted to my muddy boots placed upon the fine carpet I could only blush, distressed that I should shame Angelique by my pitiful appearance.

Mrs. Cunningham smiled a cold smile and bid Angelique show me to my room. "Palmer will unpack your things, Mary. I am sure your sister can help you find a suitable gown for dinner." With that, Angelique led me up a staircase so grand it was surely fit to reach heaven.

Palmer turned out to be a maidservant. I was anxious to do my own unpacking, but she wouldn't take the hint. I could only stand by and watch as she plucked my miserable clothes from my trunk as if they were toads. When at last I was rid of her, I looked about my room. There was a bed with a fancy coverlet and pillows, delicate chairs and dressing table, a glowing fireplace, and a window dressed in velvet drapes. From the window I could see the tops of the plane trees on the square.

Angelique came into my room with an armful of dresses and a curling iron. With a great deal of giggling and some singeing of hair we managed to decorate me so that when I went down to dinner I saw Mrs. Cunningham was relieved by my appearance.

Daniel greeted me with warmth. His great brown cow's eyes had always reminded me of Belle's and now made me lonesome for her. "Well, Mary," Daniel said, giving me a warm embrace, "we have looked forward to having you with us. I hope all is well on the island with your dear father and brother."

"And I am Mr. Cunningham, mam, and you are very welcome here," Daniel's father said to me. He was a stout, red-faced man with a hearty way about him. "We are grateful to your country for providing so delightful a daughter-in-law. If our countries had to fight one another, at least something good came out of it. I am only pleased that it did not take another war to bring you here."

We all laughed and the dinner began in a merry way. It was only when I looked down at my place that I began to worry. There were a great many odd-looking knives and forks and spoons—more than one person could possibly need. As the servants placed soup upon the table I watched to see which spoon Mrs. Cunningham took up and did the same. I could not help but think of Little Cloud and how she had struggled with our spoons and forks. I could see now how puzzled and uncertain she must have been and I was sorry I had not been more understanding.

Course after course followed. After the soup we had a delicate fish, followed by a great roast of beef, which Mr. Cunningham carved as though it had been a terrible enemy of his. The roast was followed by boiled chicken, not as tasty as my mother's recipe. The dinner ended with apple tarts and a pudding with jam.

The talk was most often about things I did not understand and people I did not know. Daniel and his father discussed what was happening far away in India, where Mr. Cunningham had once served with the British army. And there was talk of a friend who had been robbed on his way home from his club by a gang of thieves.

Mrs. Cunningham and Angelique spoke of balls and visiting. "This will all be quite new to you, Mary," Mrs. Cunningham said. "I hope we do not bore you with it. I daresay there is not much opportunity for good society on your little island."

"On the contrary, mam. We have the very best friends, all of whom would lie down and die for you if it were necessary."

"Well, my dear," Mr. Cunningham said, "I think Mary has the advantage of us. I suspect few of our social acquaintances would be so considerate. Do you count any Indians amongst your friends?"

Mrs. Cunningham frowned. "What a question, Mr. Cunningham. Of course they are not Mary's friends. What would she be doing with savages?"

In my anger I completely forgot Angelique's warning. "Yes, many are our friends," I could not help exclaiming. "White Hawk is an Indian and he is my best friend in all the world. He is no savage, for he reads and writes Latin. Also my brother is married to a Sauk chief's daughter,

Little Cloud. She is very elegant. Everyone says so. And though there are a thousand Indians on our island we can walk about at night and not be knocked on the head and robbed as you are on your island."

After this there was a very long silence. As I realized what I had done, I considered dropping to the floor and disappearing under the table.

At last Mrs. Cunningham said in a very hoarse voice, "How is it, Angelique, that you never thought to mention that your sister-in-law is an Indian?"

Before Angelique could answer, Daniel said, "Mary, I promised you a horse to ride and I will soon have one for you. You and Angelique shall ride in Hyde Park. What do you say to that?"

Hastily I expressed my gratitude. "Nothing would please me more," I told him.

Mrs. Cunningham had now composed herself. "Angelique," she said, "we must take Mary out tomorrow and get her a riding dress and whatever else a young lady might need."

Later, when Angelique and I were alone in my room, I apologized. "Angelique," I begged. "Forgive me for being so impertinent. It was only that I could not bear to hear people I love called savages."

"It was my fault, Mary. It was very wrong of me to have said nothing about Little Cloud. It was just that Mrs. Cunningham has been very kind to me and I don't like to say anything that might upset her. I am afraid that has made me into a coward," she confessed.

"Never in the world!" I told her. "Remember how we captured those terrible robbers who wanted to make off with Belle? You certainly weren't a coward then. And Mrs. Cunningham can't be nearly so nasty. Besides, there are two of us now and only one of her."

CHAPTER

10

I N THE MORNING, Mrs. Cunningham complimented me on my dress and bonnet, both of which belonged to Angelique. "I will just go along with you girls to the dressmakers," she said, "and this afternoon I mean to take you to see a picture exhibition that is opening today."

At the dressmakers I could not help but express my pleasure at the dresses ordered for me. My only misstep happened when I was so startled at learning their price I cried out without thinking, "Heavens! I could buy three pigs for that!" This amused the dressmaker but not Mrs. Cunningham.

The exhibition, by the Royal Academy of Arts, was in Somerset House, a great pile of stone with archways and wings extending every which way. The building stood beside the Thames River. I asked hopefully if we might stand by the riverbank and look out at the boats. They were numerous and of every size and shape. When Mrs. Cunningham refused, saying that the river was dirty and smelled, I followed her dutifully into the building. I was determined to be on my best behavior, for Mrs. Cunningham still treated me coldly.

As we entered the exhibition hall she said, "We must seek out many opportunities like this one, Mary, to improve your mind." Behind Mrs. Cunningham's back Angelique gave me a waggish look.

It was no chore to view the pictures. They were magnificent. In the scenes before me of countryside and sea I saw worlds so real I felt I could climb right into them and walk about.

As Angelique and I studied and exclaimed over the pictures, Mrs. Cunningham examined the people who had come to see them. She sought out the people she knew and commented on those she did not. "Lady Brug's bonnet is the very newest fashion. She has been lately in Paris. And there is young Lord Lindsay. What a fine figure of a man he is getting to be, and what a catch, though they do say he gives his father, the duke, trouble with his free-spirited ways."

Since I knew nothing of these people I paid little attention to Mrs. Cunningham's comments. I was admiring a painting of rocks and sky and water that reminded me of my own island, when a voice beside me said, "Mr. Constable. One of my favorite artists. I hope you will forgive my coming up to you so informally, Miss O'Shea, but I am greatly pleased to see you again."

"James Lindsay! Whatever are you doing here?" I exclaimed, glad to see a familiar face. "I thought you would be somewhere on the sea hanging about the topgallant crosstrees. I hope you have forgiven me for my foolish behavior. I have regretted it every day."

"I have forgiven you long since."

I was so pleased to hear this that I gave his arm a crushing squeeze. "How I miss the weevils and maggots," I said with a laugh. Then, recollecting myself, I introduced Mrs. Cunningham and Angelique.

"I am honored to make your acquaintance, madam." He turned to Angelique. "Your sister has spoken so often of you, I feel I have the pleasure of knowing you already."

As Mr. Lindsay made his formal bows I saw a look of great pleasure on Mrs. Cunningham's face. "Lord Lindsay," she said, with more warmth than I had yet heard in her voice, "it is a pleasure, I am sure. Everyone knows of your talent in making pictures. Will you not accompany us on our little tour of the exhibition? I am sure you would add much to our study."

"It would be a great privilege, madam."

I had time to look at Mr. Lindsay and saw how splendidly he was dressed. He looked quite different from the midshipman on the *Comfort*. "Can you really be *Lord* Lindsay?" I asked. "How funny."

Once again Mrs. Cunningham frowned at me. "Surely not *funny*. Lord Lindsay's father is the Duke of Oakbridge."

Mr. Lindsay's father a duke! I could hardly believe it. "But you were treated like any other midshipman," I said.

"Well, Miss O'Shea, the captain would not have a happy ship if he singled out one man in the crew over another just because he happened to have something as useless on board ship as a title."

Lord Lindsay was the perfect guide. He pointed out his favorite paintings and answered our questions. Angelique and I sometimes disagreed with his choices, so we had some merry arguments.

Me: "No cow ever looked like that!"

Angelique: "I call it very cruel to paint that woman's nose so disagreeably."

All this was said with much laughter. Mrs. Cunningham, however, never contradicted a word of Lord Lindsay's.

As we were leaving the exhibition Lord Lindsay said, "You must come and see the Thames, Miss O'Shea. If you don't know our river, you don't know our country."

Mrs. Cunningham quickly agreed. "We should like it above all things." This time she made no mention of the river being dirty and smelly. Still, she and Angelique kept back from the embankment, so I had Lord Lindsay to myself. I was relieved finally to be away from Mrs. Cunningham's disapproving frowns. "I am so glad you suggested a look at the river. I was longing to see it."

"I come here often to sketch," Lord Lindsay

confided. "There is so much life passing by."

"Will you be going to sea again?" I asked.

"No. Father has decided that with the end of the war there will be less opportunity for a naval man to advance up the line. He is sending me up to Oxford next year. There is a fine museum there at the university and pretty countryside to paint. I suppose I must open a book or two, but it will be very dull after London. However, I don't go up until after Christmas. How will you spend your time here, Miss O'Shea?"

"I want to go about and learn something of history while I am here, and Angelique's husband will get a horse for me so that I can ride in the park."

"I hope you will allow me to act as a guide for your history lesson?"

"That would be very kind of you, Lord Lindsay."

"Do please call me James! You say 'Lord Lindsay' as if I were an animal with two tails and five ears."

"Then you must call me Mary." I saw from his smile that my request pleased him.

James kindly saw us to our carriage and promised to call upon us.

His promise was the subject of our dinner

conversation. Mrs. Cunningham said to her husband and to Daniel, "You will never believe who our guide was to the exhibition. Young Lord Lindsay himself. He could not have been more kind to me and the girls. Apparently, he was an officer on the *Comfort* during Mary's journey. In fact, he seemed to take quite a fancy to Mary." She gave me a kindly smile, the first I had had from her. "I would not be surprised," she said, "if we are invited to the ball the duke and duchess are giving. I have always longed to see Lindsay House." She gave me a close look. "I daresay, Mary, you have not told Lord Lindsay about your Indian sister-in-law."

"On the contrary, mam, we had many conversations on the subject."

Mr. Cunningham smiled slyly. "You are behind the times, Mrs. Cunningham. The American, Thomas Jefferson, has written that all men are created equal. It seems your Lord Lindsay agrees. Next thing he will be renouncing his title and insisting upon being called plain 'James.'"

"Oh, sir," I said. "I do call him James."

Whereupon Mr. Cunningham and Daniel had a good laugh, but Mrs. Cunningham did not laugh at all.

A few days later the invitation to the ball arrived. After that the only talk was of dresses. Though Mrs. Cunningham and Angelique both had more dresses than they could wear out in a lifetime, Mrs. Cunningham declared that none of them would do for such an occasion. And of course, I would need something new. We made visits to shops to pluck up bolts of silk to be sent off to dressmakers. The dressmakers seemed to summon us daily for fittings. Mrs. Cunningham found fault with every seam and tuck and ruffle, so the dresses were not so much made as remade many times over.

It should have been a pleasure to look forward to an evening of dancing and good company, but the evening was spoiled for me before it even began. Mrs. Cunningham continually let me know that this was to be an opportunity for me to set my cap for James. "Of course, Lord Lindsay's parents, the duke and duchess, will have a suitable girl already selected for him, someone who can boast of a good family and a comfortable income. Still, Lord Lindsay is known for having a mind of his own, so there is a small chance for you, Mary."

"I am sure I can boast of a good family," I

said. "After all, who could be nicer than Papa and Jacques and Little Cloud and Angelique? And we have a fine farm with pigs aplenty and a cow and a bull, which is income enough for anyone. But I am not at all interested in James as a husband nor is he interested in me as anything but a friend."

Still, Mrs. Cunningham and Angelique whispered together. I was so nervous the evening of the ball that without the help and encouragement of Angelique and Palmer, I should have put everything on backward. Only the silky warmth of Little Cloud's ermine pelisse gave me any courage. When Mrs. Cunningham complimented me on its elegance I was quick to point out that it was the work of my Indian sister-in-law.

If I had been flustered before I reached Lindsay House, the sight of the great mansion was like a blow to my stomach. I could hardly catch my breath as we entered the great hall. We left off our wraps and climbed up an elegant stairway with a stream of handsomely dressed guests. At the top of the stairway our names were shouted out by a footman. I whispered to Angelique, "I shall certainly take up this custom of screaming out visitors' names when next Papa and I entertain White Hawk and the Wests."

Angelique laughed behind her fan and said, "What Elizabeth West would give to come to such a party!"

There were several hundred guests, one more elegant than the other. We followed a receiving line to greet the duke and duchess. The duke was a tall, stern-looking man who was nothing like James in his looks. The duchess, Lady Elinor, was much like James with the same gold curls and blue eyes, though there was gray in her hair, and the blue of her eyes was less the bright blue of a jay's feather and more of the faded blue of a chicory flower.

The duke barely acknowledged the bows of Mr. Cunningham and Daniel or our curtsies. Lady Elinor, however, gave us a warm greeting and took my hand in hers. "So you are the young girl from America. James tells me you were quite as important to the *Comfort*'s welfare as the captain was. I am sure we are very pleased to have you with us."

This kindness was not lost on Mrs. Cunningham, who, to my shame, exchanged a knowing look with Angelique. My embarrassment at their plotting was such that I resolved to give no sign of interest in James. When he came to claim a dance I drew away and pled first a sore ankle and then dizziness.

"What!" he exclaimed. "You look healthy as a horse. Rest if you must. I'll be back."

I saw a frown on Mrs. Cunningham's face. Angelique said, "Mary, what can you be thinking of?"

To avoid their questions I accepted the invitation to dance from a young friend of Daniel's. As we set off at a gallop I saw James glaring at me and I could not keep from blushing at my deception. I knew that I had pained him and felt so miserable I hardly heard the questions put to me by my partner. As soon as the dance ended I looked about for an escape. If I stayed I would have to put up with either Mrs. Cunningham's schemes or James's anger. Both were terrible to me.

I slipped through a doorway and found myself in a room that seemed to be built of books. Papa did not own above a dozen books, and that was considered a good showing on the island. Here it looked like all the books in the world had been gathered together. The walls were books. The tables were covered with books. I picked one up and found that it was a kind of diary kept by the duke of his fishing.

"Played fish for an hour before landing it with net. Heavy rain. Fish not rising. Fished Willow Pond."

It went on for a hundred pages or more, telling the weather and time of day and how the fish were caught. I thought of Pere Mercier and how surprised he would be to find someone had taken so much time to put down the smallest details of his fishing.

Life in London was certainly not like life on the island. I found that people did not just go ahead and do things. There were rules for everything: the way you dressed, the way you talked, the way you ate. I had to learn new rules for everything I did. I thought again of Little Cloud and how all that was natural to us was strange to her. I heartily wished I was there to tell her that at last I truly understood her feelings.

To distract myself from my longing for home, I took up a large sketchbook that lay next to the fishing diary. Turning over the pages, I was startled to see drawings of the *Comfort*. There were pictures of the crew: setting the sails, at their dances, plaiting one another's hair. Captain Hodge in all of his authority looked out from one of the pages. There were scenes of gulls flying over the empty sea. I turned a page and found myself! There were drawings of me milking the goat, and looking out over the ocean, bundled up in a rainstorm.

My face was burning. As I hurriedly turned the pages I found sketches of another girl. She was a little older than me, with an unruly tumble of curls, a thin face, and large long-lashed eyes. I thought her very lovely and hated myself for feeling jealous. I was staring down at her picture when a voice behind me said, "Why have you disappeared to waste your time with that nonsense?"

James was looking over my shoulder. "That's Sally. You ought to know her. In fact I think I will introduce you to her."

"Is she here?"

"Sally! Good heavens, no! No one here knows a thing about her. She's my secret."

My jealousy increased and I resolved to be cool to James.

"Come and dance with me and don't tell me you are dizzy."

"I'm afraid you will have to excuse me."

"I did not think you a tease, Mary. You have been the only person I know in the world who truly speaks her mind. Unless you hate me for some reason I don't understand, you had better tell me what the matter is."

I sank down on a chair and covered my face with my hands. How could I let James know that he was nothing more than a fish I was supposed to catch? I had been telling myself and Mrs. Cunningham that James was only a friend. But if that were so, why was I so upset about Sally?

James came over and gently removed my hands from my face. He knelt beside me and said, "Mary, we are good friends, are we not? Can't you tell me what is bothering you?"

I was just about to tell the truth when the duke entered the room. Catching sight of James upon his knees beside me, the duke spoke in an angry voice. "James, you are neglecting our guests and importuning this young lady with your attentions. I must ask you to go out into the ballroom and attend to your duties. And you, madam, will come with me."

James started to explain, but his father silenced him at once. I trailed after the duke while he led me to Mrs. Cunningham. I was sure she saw at once from the stormy look on the duke's face and my contrite appearance that something was amiss. Hastily she rose from her chair to greet the duke, who said only, "Madam, I hope you will forgive me if I remind you of your responsibility to this young lady. She has been left rather too much alone." He made a stiff bow and walked off, making me feel like a dead bird laid by a cat at the feet of its mistress.

Mrs. Cunningham was scarlet with embarrassment. I could hear her breathing heavily beside me. After that I was very quiet, meekly accepting offers to dance, saying little to my partners and sitting between dances with folded hands. How I wished I were back on the island dancing with White Hawk while André played his violin.

That night, when Angelique and I were alone in my room, I poured out my story.

"It is very unfortunate that the duke saw James on his knees," she said. "He will think his son was proposing and I suppose he has other plans for Lord Lindsay. I suspect it was all a little too sudden for the duke, but we mustn't give up hope."

"But I have no hopes," I insisted. "I keep trying to tell you James and I are only friends." Thinking of the picture of Sally, I said, "Anyhow, I have reason to think there is someone else for whom he cares."

Angelique appeared not to have heard me at all. "Just imagine, Mary, you might be mistress of Lindsay House someday."

I was terrified by the thought. "Never in the world! It would be like living in a prison with the duke as my jailer keeping me in chains. I hope I never see Lindsay House again."

At breakfast Mrs. Cunningham had only hard words for the ball and the duke and duchess. "They are above themselves. The duke is the rudest man I have ever met. I have nothing to say for the duchess, either. I thought her gown nearly shabby and I actually believe it had been worn on another occasion."

The rest of the morning Mrs. Cunningham hardly spoke to me. But her attitude softened considerably when at noon a carriage drew up to the door and the duchess was handed down by a coachman in an elegant livery.

The visit of Lady Elinor so flustered Mrs. Cunningham that she could hardly offer enough in the way of chairs, refreshments, and other courtesies to the duchess. Lady Elinor, however, brushed all the offers aside and said in her soft voice, "You will forgive me for calling so early, but I did not want another hour to pass by before I apologized for the duke's behavior. James was quite beside himself with embarrassment for his father. It was all a misunderstanding, which was quickly cleared up after our guests had left and James explained what had happened."

She paused for a moment before continuing. "I am afraid you will think very badly of us. Unfortunately, during the winter season the duke must stay in town and gets no fishing. When he does not fish he is not fit to live with. Of course, we hope to see all of you at Lindsay House again on a happier and less formal occasion. Now I must hurry off."

With that she bowed to each of us and, taking my hand, said kindly, "James sends his compliments, my dear." In another moment she was out of the room and into her coach.

"What a charming woman," Mrs. Cunningham said. "She is the very model of good breeding, and so fashionable." She sent a smile my way. "I believe, Mary, Lady Elinor is quite taken with you."

CHAPTER

11

January 20, 1817
Michilimackinac

Dear Mary,

How I envy you seeing so much of the world while I am chained to a desk in Mr. Astor's establishment. I write down "1 beaver skin @ 50¢." I write it down a hundred times and a hundred times more. Every animal killed and skinned across the country and brought here must be noted. I have never been so bored in my life. It was not so bad in the fall when Pere Mercier and I could get out for a little fishing or when I could help Papa with the farm. Now there is no escape.

Last year at this time I was snowshoeing across land that had no end. Every day was a surprise. In the evenings I sat around a campfire and listened to the stories of other trappers or the tales of the Indian tribe I lived with. Now of an evening there is nothing to do but sit and stare into the fireplace or join the Wests or the Sinclairs for a game of cards or a telling of stories I have heard a thousand times.

I'm afraid Little Cloud is no happier than I am. She misses her family and feels very much shut up in the house. Now that winter is here and there are only a handful of Indians on the island she hears no news of her tribe. Emma West has been very kind to her. The two of them sit together beading moccasins or embroidering petticoats, depending on whose turn it is to teach the other. Little Cloud sends her love to you.

I suppose what you really want to hear about is Belle, who misses you and moos unhappily when she sees Little Cloud or me come to milk her *instead of her mistress. Your young bull, George, is fine and getting more rambunctious all the time. Papa sends his own letter along with mine.*

You must say hello to King George III for me. Since we have beaten him twice, I don't suppose he will start another war. Give my love to Angelique and tell her she is not to become too grand a lady, since we all remember how she used to clean out the chicken coop.

Your unhappy brother,
Jacques

January 20, 1817
Michilimackinac

My dear Mary,

How I miss my youngest daughter. Everything here seems less pleasant. I do not believe I ever saw how much you did about the house and farm until you were gone. What I miss most are your cheerful ways.

I am afraid I made a mistake asking Jacques to take a position here on the island with Mr. Astor's fur business. He was not made to be shut into a room with pen and paper. He is not happy and Little Cloud is very quiet. Our house is no longer a content one. I see now that I was selfish in wanting Jacques and Little Cloud to stay here. When I was Jacques's age I left Ireland and traveled halfway around the world. Why should Jacques not do as he likes as well?

It seems very strange that I crossed the sea in one direction and you crossed it in another. I hope you will not take too much to British ways. I have tried very hard to be a good Christian and forgive the British for what they do in Ireland, but I still have a way to go.

Give Angelique my love and tell her we miss her. And Mary, do not be too long in returning. The days without you are very long.

Your loving Papa

February 2, 1817
Detroit

Dear Mary,

The winter here has been severe. The Detroit River is frozen over. There is a shortage of food.

Many of the horses have had to be killed because there is nothing for them to eat. Even wood for heating is scarce and the French are staying up at night to protect the trees in their orchards.

Governor Cass wishes to make Michigan a state. To increase the value and size of the territory he is set upon buying more land from the Indians. He deals only with those few chiefs who would sell out their tribe for a little money and liquor. The great majority of chiefs who don't wish to sell are being betrayed. Speculators buy the land from the Indians for half a cent an acre and resell it for fifteen dollars. I do what I can, but my age and lack of position are against me.

Now I have to make a decision. I have been offered a teaching position by Pere Richard at one of his schools. If I accept his offer I will be tied to Detroit. There would be little opportunity of returning either to Michilimackinac or to my people on L'Arbre Croche. Mary, how I wish you were here so that I could talk with you about this. I try to think of you in London in fine clothes in a fine house and with fine people. It does not seem to be my Mary. Surely you were made to tramp through the woods and along the shores of the island and not for London's

drawing rooms and ballrooms. Luckily I have
many pictures in my mind of you on the island.
I hope you will not be too long away.

> *With kindest regards,*
> *White Hawk*

CHAPTER

12

SEVERAL WEEKS went by and I did not see James, although I had a letter from him saying that he was up at Oxford at Balliol College. "The lectures give me time to practice my sketching. I look forward to Easter and a return to civilization."

It was Easter week when Daniel said he had found a horse for me to ride. On the island I had ridden in an old pair of Papa's breeches. Now Angelique was fastening me into long, sweeping skirts and a ruffled shirt, and placing a tall hat upon my head.

"However can I ride in such an outfit? I won't be able to get my legs over the horse."

"Of course not, Mary. Here women ride sidesaddle, not astride. You will learn in no time at all."

"Why aren't you coming, Angelique?"

Angelique blushed. "I can't tell you now, Mary. I promise to tell you tomorrow."

In my eagerness to see my horse I thought no more about Angelique's mystery, supposing it to have something to do with preparations for yet another dinner or ball.

Daniel, handsome in his high hat and shiny boots, accompanied me to Hyde Park, where we set out for Rotten Row, the bridle path that ran along a pretty lake called the Serpentine.

The March day was crisp with a bright sun and a brisk wind. I tied my hat on with a scarf. I was given a lesson in riding sidesaddle by the groom, Wigson, and warned that my horse, Ginger, was lively. Ginger was a bay with a white star on her nose. Her mane was braided and her tail clubbed. In my fondest dreams I had never thought to have my own horse. I could not leave off patting Ginger's neck or speaking sweet words to her. My only regret was that I was not riding the trails through the woods of Michilimackinac, for I did not feel at home with the crowds of elegantly dressed riders.

Many of the riders on the trail were known to Daniel. The men doffed their hats and the women nodded and smiled. Our pace was lazy, for we had to hack along very slowly to keep from disturbing the other leisurely riders. I longed for a good gallop and I felt sure Ginger did as well.

We were halfway along the path when I heard someone call out, "Mary, wait!" I turned to see James on a great chestnut-and-gray mount. We rode side by side while Daniel dropped behind us.

"Mary, I am happy for the chance of apologizing for my father's behavior at the ball. I hope you were not offended."

"It was my own foolish behavior that caused it all. I surely don't blame your father."

James smiled with relief. "Now you must tell me what you have seen of London."

I named the sights the Cunninghams had guided me to, especially the Tower of London and Westminster Abbey. "But most of our time is spent in making calls upon people and sitting up very straight in uncomfortable chairs and talking a great deal about nothing at all."

"If I could find a means of spiriting you away from the Cunninghams while I'm down on vacation, I could show you another part of London. We could see the docks where there is no elegance but much life, and I'd show you Limehouse. Only I'm afraid the Cunninghams would not wish to go where I want to take you and they would never allow you to go about alone with me."

"Why ever not? Why should I not be trusted with you?"

"I am sure it would be so. Ask your brother-in-law if you doubt me."

I held back my horse and while James rode on ahead I kept pace with Daniel. "James has asked me to go with him to see the docks and Limehouse. Surely that would be all right?"

"Mary, what can you be thinking of?" Daniel frowned. "It would be unheard of for you to go about alone with Lord Lindsay. Especially to such dangerous places. I wonder that he even suggested it."

"I ran all over the island with White Hawk," I reminded him.

"London is not Michilimackinac. We do not have such free and easy ways."

Just then Daniel noticed two fashionably dressed women sitting on a bench along the Row. He reined in his horse to chat with his friends while I once again joined James.

"You were right," I said. "I'm a prisoner."

"Could you not escape for a few hours?"

It was said in the same tone of voice he used when he had called out to the midshipmen, "We could dress her up like us!" Thinking of what had happened on that occasion, I was wary. Still, I hated the thought of coming so far and seeing so little. On impulse I said, "Meet me in Berkeley Square tomorrow morning at eleven. On Mondays Mrs. Cunningham and Angelique return visits all day. I'll find a way to stay home. Now I'll race you to the end of the lake." With that I dug my heels into Ginger and urged her on.

We flew by the elegant and lazy riders, scattering them like so many leaves and ending in a breathless tie and a fit of laughter. I swallowed my laughter ·quickly, though, when I saw Daniel's angry frown. James and I apologized and I was led off in disgrace.

By teatime Mrs. Cunningham had already heard from her friends about my misbehavior. As she poured, there was a very tight smile on her face. "My dear Mary, you must recall that you are not in the wilds of America. Your escapade was the talk of Rotten Row. Fortunately it was with Lord Lindsay, who is known for his spirited ways, so we can forgive you for being led astray by him."

"It wasn't his fault, mam. I challenged him. I thought it a shame to waste such a pleasant afternoon and such a strong horse."

Mrs. Cunningham looked very severe. I was feeling very miserable until Mr. Cunningham kindly cheered me by saying, "I know just what you mean, Mary. I would as soon ride a wooden rocking horse as hack up and down Rotten Row."

In the morning, before I could make some excuse to stay at home, Mrs. Cunningham said, "Angelique and I have a special call to make, Mary. It's best you remain here today."

My curiosity about the "special call" lasted only a moment, for I was mightily relieved not to have to make up a fib so that I could make my escape and join James. As soon as the Cunninghams' carriage rounded the corner I put on my jacket and bonnet and hurried down the stairway.

Palmer appeared just as I was getting ready to slip out the doorway. "Why, miss," she said, looking surprised. "Are you thinking of going out by yourself?"

Hastily I said, "Surely a turn in the square would do no harm, Palmer."

She appeared uncertain but said only, "I'll just get you one of madam's warm shawls to wrap over your jacket. There's a cold wind blowing." A paisley shawl of the finest wool was placed over my shoulders and I was allowed to go on my way.

Overhead the clouds were herded along the blue sky like flocks of sheep. In the square the few dead leaves that still clung to the plane trees rattled and rustled. The grasses were white and brittle and the daffodils shriveled by the late frost. James was sitting on a bench beating his arms to keep warm. When he saw me, he sprang up and guided me to a handsome coach with the Lindsay arms painted upon the door. We rattled along at a great pace until James knocked on the roof of the carriage to signal the coachman above to stop.

I looked about me at a world I could never have imagined. We were alongside the Thames, surrounded by great blocks of buildings fashioned of red brick. A thousand men of many different colors and costumes ran about loading and unloading the sailing ships along the wharves. On the docks were heaps of bales, stacks of hides, and long rows of casks. There were ships of all sizes and shapes, their names spelled out in every language on earth. "James, where are we?"

"These are the London docks. The West India Docks are over there and the East India Docks there. And just in that direction is Execution Dock, where pirates used to be hanged in chains. I never tire of sketching here. Just think of what these warehouses hold: spices from Africa, tea from India, tobacco from America, wine from France, even gold and silver and diamonds. The whole world seems to end up on these docks."

Apart from some curious glances, the dock-workers were too busy with their tasks to pay much attention to us. A few waved a quick greeting to James, whom they appeared to recognize. It was very different at our next stop.

James directed the coachman to take us to Limehouse. I saw the man frown and hesitate, but at last we sped away. The distance from the London docks was short. As he opened the door for us the coachman said in a warning voice,

"M'lord, are you quite certain this is where you wish to take the young lady?"

In a majestic voice James said, "I quite know where I want to be, Davis. Stay here. We'll be back shortly." James took up a package from the carriage and led me away with him.

Davis had a look on his face that suggested he smelled something quite bad. Indeed, as I got out I noticed the odor myself, but it was soon forgotten as a crowd of dirty children in tattered clothes swarmed around us begging for pennies. Ahead of us was a filthy lane. James took my arm and guided me past a row of crumbling hovels, boxlike shelters no larger than eleven or twelve feet wide and deep. Faces peered out from each house. Gaping windows and doors let in the cold. The luckier residents burned a small fire of charcoal.

I plucked up my skirts and petticoats, for the lane was a cesspool of raw sewage and the stench was almost unbearable. A drunken man lurched at us. A woman, also drunk, shouted curses at a child who clutched at her. The woman pushed the child to the ground. I clung to James, who moved along through the crowd of children, taking no notice of the oaths sent our way.

I did not like to look into the houses, for I did

not want to be staring at the misfortune of others, yet I could not help myself. James led me toward a hovel that seemed like all of the others. The outside walls were covered with soot and mold. "The Thames floods in the spring," he said, "and creeps into these huts, soaking everything. The sun never seems to find its way here long enough to dry things out."

This was a very different London from the one I had been shown. On our island, when people were in want, everyone saw and helped. Here, it appeared no one wished to see and no one helped.

As we entered the house I saw that it was better fitted out than the others I had glimpsed. There was a door to open and shut. Inside, two candles threw light upon some sticks of furniture. A thin, sickly man lay on a dirty cot. Even in the dim light I could see his pale body shivering beneath a thin sheet. Sitting beside him on a broken stool was a girl not much older than I. Though her face was streaked with dirt and her hair a tangled bird's nest of curls, I was startled to see that she was the pretty girl in James's sketchbook. Clinging to her was a toddler who had fastened her eyes upon the package James carried. The mother's prettiness was spoiled by an angry, sullen look. Her voice, when she addressed James, was accusing. "You've not been here for a week, m'lord." *M'lord* was said in a mocking way.

"I'm sorry, Sally, I couldn't get away." Hastily James handed the package to the girl. "It is only what food I could get out of the kitchen. Some pies and a joint of mutton and a little port for Thomas to keep up his strength." James turned to the sick man. "Thomas, how are you feeling?"

For an answer the young man half rose in bed, which caused him to begin coughing in such a terrible way that I thought his whole insides might tumble out. At last he fell back upon the cot. "Well, sir, I'm good as can be expected. I suppose we all have our troubles. One of the men from the *Comfort* stopped by the other day and said Captain Hodge was without a ship, there not being enough ships to go around these days. It's a terrible thing when a country can't find a war to keep its ships in the water and its sailors at work."

James explained to me, "Thomas sailed on the *Comfort* with us a couple of years ago. You couldn't find a better hand."

I asked, "Is there no other work for you, Thomas, besides the navy?"

"Well, there's not enough of me these days to manage a job, miss."

James said, "Thomas was unlucky enough to have a cannon break loose in a storm and roll his way. I'm afraid it crushed his legs."

I saw now that under the ragged sheet the man's body stopped at his upper legs. I was so taken aback, I hardly knew what to say. Something about Thomas's grim, stubborn expression suggested easy words of sympathy would not be welcome.

"You don't have your drawing things, m'lord," Sally said. There was blame in her voice.

"No, but you shall have your money all the same." James turned to me. "Sally and her daughter are two of my favorite models. Now, Tom, what have you made for me this week?"

"It's right here, sir."

I exclaimed as he held out a perfectly carved ship, a model of the *Comfort* with its masts rigged with sails. It was correct in all its details, even down to the figurehead.

"Sally and me could hardly believe the money you got for us for the last one, sir."

"And I have orders for as many as you can make. Here is the payment for this one."

Thomas seemed delighted with the sum of

money given him by James, but Sally said, "It don't seem much for all the hours he puts into those ships. The last of the money went for a doctor and food."

"I could have done without the doctor," Thomas said. "I was that weak after he bled me. I wanted Sally to spend the money on a shawl to keep her warm."

"Warm shawls aren't for the likes of me," Sally said, looking resentfully at my shawl.

I found myself saying, "You needn't buy a shawl. You can have this one. We have more at home." I put the shawl about her shoulders and she gave me a brilliant smile.

"Oh, miss, thank you. Now, if I had a bonnet like yours I believe I could be quite happy."

She looked so hungrily at my bonnet that I would have given it to her had James not stopped me. "Now, Sally, you would not have Miss O'Shea travel about London bareheaded. We must go now, but I'll be back before I return to Oxford."

Sally's lovely mouth was shaped into a pout. "I'm sure I don't see why a grown man should be playing at school. What's to become of us while you are away?"

James assured her he would see that they

were taken care of, and after a final cheering word to Thomas, we left.

James was apologetic. "You must not mind Sally. I would rather have her insolent than cringing. She has very little to make her happy."

He helped me into the coach. "Now we shall have to make *you* happy. I have a more cheerful place in mind."

The coach took us along the Ratcliffe Highway, where there was much to see. On either side of the road were meeting places for sailors, mission halls, chapels, churches, and countless taverns. There were shops for every kind of ship's need, from cordage to lanterns. At one place men were gathered at a doorway, a strange look upon their faces. "Opium dens," James said. "The poor fools spend their last penny there for the drug. It is a kind of living death."

I shuddered and turned away.

The coach stopped once more and this time Davis seemed almost eager to hand me out. "A most interesting place, mam," he said approvingly.

We entered a kind of warehouse. Over the doorway hung the sign, CHARLES JAMRACH, NATURALIST.

"He's the largest dealer in wild animals any-where in the world," James said. I believed it, for as soon as we entered the building the violent animal odor nearly suffocated us. "Jamrach will sell you a dozen lions or a boxful of giraffes or as many boa constrictors as you wish."

There was room after room of cages, both mammoth and tiny. I saw my first elephant and my first dormouse. There were monkeys swing-ing about and pacing tigers. There were kanga-roos from New South Wales and buffalo from America. One room was full of bright green par-rots flying about. "Who buys these creatures?" I asked.

"Wild animal parks, circuses, and eccentrics who like to have a tiger or two about them."

At that moment we came to a small cage and I heard a familiar sound, a kind of hoarse screech. An eagle was huddled inside the cage, one fierce eye staring out at me. I could not help bursting into tears. I thought of the eagles that soared over Michilimackinac and I pitied the captive. I mourned for all the hundreds and hun-dreds of wild animals that had been stolen from their homes and shut into cages in this dreadful place. I thought of Sally and Thomas, shut into their dark house, and Angelique, shut into Mrs.

Cunningham's cage of manners. At that moment I would have given anything to be back on my island running through the woods with White Hawk, with the pitiful eagle free and soaring overhead and with no one to tell me how I must behave.

I saw that my tears had distressed James and spoiled his pleasure. Hastily I apologized, explaining about the eagle.

He sighed. "I quite understand. It is no different with me. All I want in the world is to be left alone to make pictures that show people a little of the world they would never otherwise see—pleasant things and things that are not so pleasant. My parents will not hear of it. As soon as I have finished with Oxford, or more likely, Oxford has finished with me, I am to take over my father's duties managing Castle Oakbridge. Even there I might do some good with the tenants, but Papa will be watching over my shoulder to see that nothing is changed."

James left me off at Berkeley Square only minutes before Angelique and Mrs. Cunningham were due to return. Palmer greeted me with a worried expression. "Oh, miss, where have you been? I was that worried." She was startled at my appearance. "Heavens, miss, look at the nasty mud on your boots. You smell something terrible, like a stable. You had better hurry out of your things before madam returns. I'll send up some hot water for your bath." She gave me a worried look. "Where is the mistress's shawl?"

I blushed, suddenly aware of what I should have known at the time—that the shawl was not mine to give away. "I must have left it in the square, Palmer."

Clearly she did not believe me. "I'll send out a footman to look, but you can be sure it will be gone by now. Let's hope the madam doesn't ask for it."

CHAPTER

13

AT FIRST NO NOTICE was taken of the missing shawl, for we heard something startling at dinner. As the pheasant cutlets were being passed around, Mrs. Cunningham announced, "We have very happy news to tell."

At this Angelique blushed and murmured, "But mam, I had hoped to tell Daniel myself and my sister too." I was startled to see tears forming in her eyes.

Daniel started to say, "Mother, perhaps we

should let Angelique—" but his mother interrupted him.

"Nonsense, my dear, it is an event that concerns us all. Of course, it is still early and the news must stay with the family."

Considering that there was a butler and two footmen in the dining room I thought that unlikely. However, the Cunninghams thought no more of the presence of servants than if they had been wooden statues.

"After our visits today," Mrs. Cunningham went on, "we stopped in Harley Street to see Dr. Meechum. There is to be another Cunningham."

For a moment there was silence. I thought at first a cousin or uncle was coming to visit. A glance at Angelique's flushed face told me otherwise. Daniel sprang out of his chair and went to her. "A baby!" he said. "My dear, this is happy news indeed." Mr. Cunningham offered his hearty congratulations.

I reached for Angelique's hand and squeezed it. She smiled at me. "You will be Aunt Mary."

"Come," Mrs. Cunningham said. "There is a dinner to be eaten and plans to be made. We must have a name for the boy."

"What if it isn't a boy?" I asked.

"Of course it will be a boy," Mrs. Cunningham

answered. "He must be called Edgebolton. That was Daniel's grandfather's name. It would be very suitable."

In a quiet voice Angelique said, "I had thought to call him Matthew after my father, mam."

"But he will be a Cunningham, not an O'Shea. There can be no question. What do you say, Mr. Cunningham?"

"Well, the name would certainly do my father honor, but the important thing for a boy is the school. He must go to Broadcroft. All the Cunninghams go there. And no mollycoddling. He must be sent off as soon as he turns seven, just as Daniel was. It is the making of a boy."

Angelique was looking more and more upset. "But sir," she said, "Daniel has told me the sorriest tales about Broadcroft. He was made to take a cold bath every morning and break the ice in the tub to do it. He was often beaten by the tutors and the food was little beside thin soup and gruel."

"Exactly so," Mr. Cunningham said. "Just the thing to turn a boy into a man, eh, Daniel?"

"Well, sir, I would say I became a man *in spite* of the rigors of Broadcroft."

"We are putting the cart before the horse," Mrs. Cunningham said. "The first thing we must do is find a nursemaid to care for the baby. I have heard Mrs. Conrad speak very well of a woman they had, a strong-willed woman who put up with no interference in the nursery. I'll see her in the morning. She is much in demand, so the sooner we engage her the better."

I heard myself asking, "Is Angelique not to have any say in this?"

Mrs. Cunningham gave me a freezing look. "She is having the baby, Mary. That is quite enough."

That evening Angelique crept into my room. Throwing herself onto the bed, she began to sob. Between sobs she said, "They have taken my baby away from me and I have not even had it yet."

I put my arms around her. "Angelique, you and Daniel must break free from the Cunninghams. You must have your own house, even if it is nothing more than a hovel."

"It needn't be a hovel. Daniel has money left to him from his aunt. We could have a very pleasant little house. It is just that the Cunninghams won't let us leave."

"They can't stop you, surely. You are not prisoners." Although as I said it I was not so sure.

"You must get Daniel to talk with his parents tomorrow."

I remembered all the sad captured and caged animals at Charles Jamrach's warehouse and resolved that this was one cage I would open. If Angelique would not speak up to the Cunninghams, I would.

The discovery of my foolishness the next morning made that impossible. Mr. and Mrs. Cunningham were busy with plans for the baby. Angelique and Daniel were silent, exchanging quick secret looks with one another. I was trying to get up my courage to speak my mind.

But I had no opportunity, for as soon as breakfast was over Mrs. Cunningham began preparations for her visit to Mrs. Conrad to see about the nursemaid. She called to Palmer. "Bring me my paisley shawl."

My heart sank. A flustered Palmer appeared. "I'm sorry, madam, it doesn't seem to be in its place." There was a quick look at me. "I can't think where it might be."

"Look again, Palmer. You are very careless."

The minute Palmer was out of the room, Mrs. Cunningham said, "It would not surprise me to find one of the servants had stolen it."

I took a deep breath and in a shaking voice

said, "It was not the servants, mam, it was me. I gave it away."

Mrs. Cunningham's shriek of surprise brought Daniel and Mr. Cunningham into the hall. "What can you be saying, girl?" she demanded.

"It was for a poor woman in Limehouse who was very cold. She asked for it and I hadn't the heart to refuse."

"What's this?" Mr. Cunningham said. "Mary, I cannot believe you have been in a place like Limehouse."

I had to tell the entire story. "Please don't blame James," I finished. "I asked to see something of London besides drawing rooms that all look alike. It was my fault. I promise to buy another one. Papa gave me a five-dollar gold piece."

Mrs. Cunningham scowled at me. "You don't know what you are saying. The wool in my shawl was so fine I could draw it through a ring. A five-dollar gold piece would not buy an inch of that shawl. But it is not the shawl we must be concerned about," she continued. "I wonder why we were foolish enough to ask you to visit us. You have caused us nothing but embarrassment with your forward ways. I cannot think Lord

Lindsay would have suggested such an adventure without your insisting upon it. You are a very poor influence on Angelique. Now that she is about to have our baby we must protect her from any such influences."

Mr. Cunningham said, "Come, my dear, you are being a little harsh on Mary, are you not? This is just high spirits. I am sure she meant no harm in her adventures about London. As for the shawl, it is easily replaced."

I could not think of a word to say, but Angelique, the most mild-mannered creature on earth, stood up very tall and very angry. "Mary has ever been a good influence on me. When some evil men might have killed our cow it was Mary who urged me to take it into our house so that we saved it. She worked day and night to keep the farm while our father was away. She hoed all day in the hot sun when I would not because I cared too much for my complexion. She cleaned out the cow shed and saw to the pigs and I daresay none of the women we visit, no matter how fine, would do as much."

Mrs. Cunningham could only stare open-mouthed at Angelique as she took a breath and went on: "If Mary is not welcome here, neither am I. Daniel and I will find our own place. I will take care of our baby myself, and no one will send him to a school where they starve and beat him just because his father and grandfather were starved and beaten."

Mr. Cunningham was taken aback. "I am sure Mrs. Cunningham did not mean her words unkindly," he faltered. "Mary's adventure was only a lark. We quite understand—no one will send her away. Now let's have no more talk of moving out."

Daniel was at Angelique's side with his arm tightly about her. His cow's eyes that were usually so mild were flashing. "Angelique is quite right. It is natural for a family to wish to set up their own house. Of course we appreciate all you have done for us, but with a child coming we must have our own home. As to Mary, I can tell you to speak to the British commander of Fort Michilimackinac. He will give her a splendid character reference."

It was plain from the stricken look on Mrs. Cunningham's face that she saw that her ill nature had driven her son from her home and Angelique from her control. For a moment I felt almost sorry for her. Then I considered what it would be to have a nephew called Edgebolton.

CHAPTER

14

 EACH DAY ANGELIQUE, Daniel, and I would set out to look for a suitable house. At the end of a day's unsuccessful search we returned to the Cunninghams full of unhappiness. Mr. Cunningham said over and over, "I don't know what you can be thinking of, Daniel, to leave so comfortable a situation. You have everything you could want here."

Mrs. Cunningham went about with a most melancholy air, hardly speaking at all. I believe she blamed me for what was happening, for her most resentful looks were aimed my way. At the dinner table everyone was so polite it was close to murder. It was May when a house was finally found and Daniel, Angelique, and I began our move from Berkeley Square.

As the trunks were carried out, Mrs. Cunningham sat in the drawing room, sometimes sobbing and sometimes scolding the footmen for carelessness with the trunks.

Mr. Cunningham had chosen to be away rather than see our departure. The night before he had privately assured us that Mrs. Cunningham would forgive us. "I can promise you when the baby comes she will not stay away."

Before we left, Daniel kissed his mother and said, "Believe me, mam, it is for the best."

Angelique said, "We want you to be our first guest, mam."

I thanked Mrs. Cunningham for her kindness in having me. Her only answer to the three of us was to burst into fresh sobs. We left with heavy hearts.

The trip across London to Daniel and Angelique's new home was a sad one. It was only when we turned into St. John's Wood and saw the little redbrick house with its fresh white trim that our spirits rallied. St. John's Wood was a new settlement with modest houses. King James had once hunted deer there and there were still wooded paths to wander down. Daniel and Angelique's new home was the neatest little house in the world. The rooms were tiny but held everything that was wanted. The whole house would nearly have fit into the sitting room of Lindsay Hall, but size did not matter to Angelique. "It is so strange, Mary," she said. "When I first came to London I thought nothing would please me more than a grand house and servants. Now I would not trade our little house with its freedom for all of Windsor Castle."

We were only a week in the house when an invitation arrived in the mail from James's mother, Lady Elinor.

My dear Mary,

The duke and I would be so pleased if you could join us at Castle Oakbridge for a fortnight. Spring here is pleasant and you should not end your visit to England without seeing some of its countryside. It will be a family affair, so we shall be quite cozy. Make us happy by saying you will come.

Elinor,
Duchess of Oakbridge

Angelique was delighted with the invitation. "Of course you must go, Mary. It is very kind of the duchess."

"But how can you be cozy in a castle? I don't want to be among such grand people. What would I wear? What would I say?"

"It only *used* to be a castle. Now it is just a large home. And I will give you whatever clothes you need. As for what you should say, I have never known you to be at a loss for words. And James will be there to keep you company."

With Angelique's help I sent a very pretty acceptance note to the duchess. Early in June the Lindsay coach carried me to Castle Oakbridge. Driving down a tree-lined entrance well over a mile long, I came upon the castle gradually. From a distance the great stone building appeared small. As we drew closer and closer the castle became larger and larger until it seemed to be everywhere.

James was there to greet me. "Well, Mary,

what do you say to Castle Oakbridge?"

"James, it's such a huge place! There must be a thousand rooms."

"Not above two hundred," James said, leading me inside. "Small, as castles go. Most of the rooms are shut up. It's a drafty old place. In the winter if you are more than a foot from a fireplace you have to wear coats and gloves and a stocking cap pulled over your ears." The picture of the duke and duchess in such hats made me forget my nervousness and I found myself laughing.

Lady Elinor hurried to greet me. "You are very welcome, my dear. We have been looking forward to your visit. James will show you about later. Now you must have time to dress. Dinner will be served in an hour. I'll take you to your room myself."

Angelique had warned me that formal dress would be expected for evening meals. Indeed, though we were only four at the dining table we were all dressed as though we were attending a great ball. I worried constantly that I would spill soup on Angelique's fine dress. The table could easily have seated fifty people, so we were very distant one from another. To be heard our voices had to be raised to a loud pitch.

"James," the duke said, "I have just had a new horse sent over from our stable in Ireland. He's a chestnut gelding, sixteen hands, deep chest, sturdy limbs. He'll make a fine hunter. You might give him a try when you and Mary go out for a ride."

"You have a farm in Ireland, sir?" I asked. "I did not know you were Irish."

"Irish!" The duke laughed. "Indeed not. A very barbaric people. Still, they know their horses."

Lady Elinor hastily said, "Come, my dear, I am sure there are some very fine Irish—and our guest and her family among them."

The duke flushed. "Yes, yes, I apologize. I did not think. It is just that they are a stubborn lot. We have allowed them into Parliament and that is still not good enough for them."

James said, "Mary is probably too polite to point out that there are only one hundred members of Parliament from Ireland and six hundred fifty-eight from England. No bill favorable to Ireland will be passed under such conditions."

I could not be still. "It is not just that," I said. "The British own half the island. When an Irish farmer improves his place the British landowner raises his rent so that he loses his land. That happened in my papa's family and Papa had to go to America."

The duke bristled. "I can assure you, mam, my agent treats the Irish who farm my land quite fairly."

"I hope you are there often, sir, to see that that is so." Papa had told many stories of cruel agents who did as they wished and were never checked by the absent British landlord.

James said, "Mary has you there, sir. I don't believe you have crossed to Ireland in some months."

The duke's face was very red. Just as he was about to scold James, Lady Elinor spoke up. "Come, there is no chance we will solve at dinner what has not been settled in four hundred years. Let us find out what would please Mary while she is here." She turned to me. "What would you say to a ball in your honor?"

I hastily answered, "Oh, mam, that is very kind of you, but what I would really enjoy would be a look at your animals."

The duchess was puzzled. "Animals?"

"James tells me you have a large working farm with cows and pigs and sheep. We have no sheep on our island and I would like to find out if sheep would survive our cold weather."

The duke forgot his anger. "Now, there is a sensible girl. I will give you a tour of the farm myself, for James only knows how to draw animals. He has no idea in the world of what they are for. We have some Shropshire sheep that would be just the thing for you. They will give you good wool and tasty mutton and can manage on a sparse pasture. Just right for your island. A pretty sheep, too, with a dark face and no horns to bother with. You shall see them first thing in the morning, and anything else you like as well."

The duke and I got on very well the next morning. He gave me a pair of boots, told me to tuck up my skirts, and led me to the barns.

After lunch was over the duke suggested we visit a nearby market. "I'm going to buy some Oxford sheep. They have a fine, heavy fleece and the lambs grow before your very eyes."

James said, "Now, Father, please remember Mary is my guest and you are not to have her all to yourself. I want to show her around the house."

I was carried away by James to explore the castle. We went up and down two dozen stairways, into great halls where you could hardly see up to the ceiling, and dark dungeons where James said prisoners had moldered away leaving only a heap of bones. The furnishings were on such a grand scale, with chairs so like thrones, that I felt no larger than a doll sitting in them. Many of the rooms actually had names, as if they were people: the King James bedroom, Queen Mary's parlor, the first duke's library. The castle was full of hundreds of years of history.

There was so much to explore in the castle and on its grounds, the days were pleasantly spent. The duke often included me on his rounds of the farm. James and I rode for miles through the countryside. Occasionally Lady Elinor would invite me to accompany her on her visits to the tenants on their estate. She carried food for those who were having a hard time of it and medicines for the ill, whom she gently nursed. She was kindness itself, but I always felt uncomfortable on those visits and thought that the tenants would have been happier had they owned their own land and could buy for themselves what the duchess so generously gave.

James and I had a favorite place. We climbed a narrow winding stairway to a small door that opened onto the roof of the castle. I inched out a bit at a time to the very edge. James would bring his sketchbook and we would settle down on the sun-warmed tiles of the roof, James to draw and me to wonder at what I saw before me.

On the last afternoon of my visit, as I was looking out at the castle grounds, James asked, "What do you think of all that?"

For an answer I could only sigh. Below me was the castle's vast park with its newly leafed trees, flowering gardens, and lakes. There were pastures with cows and fields dotted with sheep and their lambs. The duke and duchess owned not only acres of land but a whole village with houses and people.

"How can it be fair for one family to possess so much, James?"

"Our property has been handed down from generation to generation. I suppose we could sell it so that it could be divided up into little plots and hundreds of houses put upon it, but I am not sure that would be any better. Also, Father and Mother take very good care of the people who live on our land."

"What if they should have a cruel landlord?"

"That's not likely."

"What will happen when your father dies?"

"It will all be mine—or rather, I will belong to

the castle and the land, for Father must work from dawn to dusk to hold it all together."

I could believe that. I had seen the steady procession of gamekeepers, gardeners, dairymen, grooms, and carpenters that moved in and out of the duke's office while the duchess was busy with the butler and cook and countless maids.

"Will you like that, James?"

James put down his sketchbook and looked at me in a strange way. "I might, if I could share it with the right person."

"Heavens, I am sure any girl would like to live in such a paradise. Of course, she would have to put up with you." I grinned.

"Would you, Mary?"

"Would I what?" I was beginning to feel nervous.

"Would you live here at Castle Oakbridge and put up with me?"

I suddenly began to feel very uncomfortable. I would have escaped, but I did not see how I could jump off the roof. Instead, I simply said, "I am here now and enjoying my visit very much."

"Mary, don't play games with me. I want you to marry me."

I looked to see if it was a very long fall. It was.

The little door that led down the stairs was far away. Besides, James had taken my hand and was hanging on to me.

I took a deep breath. "James, I shouldn't know how to behave in such a life. I should do and say all the wrong things."

"You should do just as you wish. You needn't sit about embroidering all day. If you like I could fire the swineherd and you could take care of the goats and pigs as you did on the ship."

"James, don't tease me. I am truly fond of you, but you would soon see all my faults."

"Mary, I love you for your faults, for they are not faults at all. You are fair and honest and plain-spoken. There is not another girl like you in all England."

He paused a moment before going on. "I can see I have surprised you. You needn't give me your answer today. Only promise to think about what I have said, for I love you, Mary." To cover his embarrassment he quickly said, "Now I suppose we had better go for a good gallop."

Eagerly I got up, and as soon as I had hurried into my riding clothes we were cantering over fields and all the awkwardness was gone. As we rode along I thought how much I enjoyed being with James and what pleasure there would be in living in so magical a place. Yet, it was not *my* place as Michilimackinac was my place. All the history was another country's history.

I would have a great deal at Castle Oakbridge. I would even be a duchess one day. But I would lose Papa and Jacques and Little Cloud. And White Hawk. Thinking of White Hawk, my mind went flying home. On the island I never had to worry about what I wore or what I did. Everyone was my friend, rich or poor. I did not think I would ever be able to talk with James as I talked with White Hawk, for James had a way of turning serious things into some foolishness.

It had been hard enough being away from Papa for nearly a year. He was always in my thoughts. I did not see how I could leave my island forever. Still, I could not forget how Papa had given the farm to Jacques. It would never be mine—no matter how long I stayed. That had changed everything.

After supper each evening James and his father stayed on in the dining room for a glass of port and a talk about the estate. The duke never ceased to hope that James would begin to take an interest in the land. Lady Elinor and I would sit with our coffee and tell one another what we had done all day. On this evening I was uncomfortable with her, for I could not help but think of James's proposal.

As if she could read my mind, the duchess said, "Mary, I hope you will forgive me for speaking plainly about you and James, but I think plain speaking is what you like."

At this I smiled, but I felt nervous. It is one thing to speak plainly to someone, but it is another thing to have someone speak plainly to you.

Lady Elinor reached over and took my hand in hers. "I have to confess I have been scheming. I know my son well and when I first saw the two of you together I could see that James cared for you. Because of that I wanted to know you better. That is why I invited you to Castle Oakbridge. Since you have been here we have all come to love you.

"I will be honest with you, Mary. As fond as the duke and I are of you, we have a selfish reason for wishing to see a marriage between you and James. In the past James could talk only of running off to the ends of the earth in search of subjects for his art. He was always ready to sail on the next ship rather than settle down here. Since he has met you, we have seen a change.

We believe that if he was married to you he would be willing to take up the responsibilities of the estate. And you would be of great help to him with your knowledge of animals and your love of the land."

I did not know what to say. Lady Elinor saw how flustered I was, and said, "I hope you will forgive me for speaking out, Mary."

"Oh, yes, mam. You and the duke have been so kind to me, and I am fond of James. It is just that I am so far from home. I don't see how I can make up my mind without talking to my papa. England is such a distance from so many of the people I love. And what if I should embarrass you and the duke? All of this is so new to me."

"My dear, the only people who would be embarrassed by you would be people who place no value on honesty and frankness. The opinion of such people does not matter to me."

We heard the door to the dining room open. The duchess let go of my hand and quickly said, "Let this be between us. You will be going back to London tomorrow and we will see you there. I don't wish to hurry you; I only wanted you to know how welcome you would be as our daughter-in-law."

I could not sleep that night. I could not pretend

to be entirely surprised at James's affection for me. For myself, I *was* very fond of James. I was pleased, too, that the duchess thought me a suitable wife for James. Even the duke did not seem to entirely hate me and no longer blamed me for what had happened at the ball. Yet their reason for wishing me to marry James did not seem a good one. Like Mrs. Cunningham and Angelique, they wanted me to catch him as though he were a fox to be hunted down. It was even worse with James's parents, for they wanted me not only to trap James but to serve as his jailer so that he would be tied to the castle like one of the prisoners whose bones were found in the dungeons.

If James and I married, things might be well for a few years, but someday James might blame me for keeping him from doing what he wanted to, just as Jacques blamed Papa for keeping him from the life he longed for. I wished that I were on Michilimackinac again so that I could walk alone along the shore of the island. It seemed the only place in the whole world where everything was clear and simple.

The next morning I thanked the duke and duchess. There were tender good-byes all around and promises of an early reunion. As

James helped me into the coach, he pressed my hand. As I said good-bye to him I was as uncertain as ever. If I returned to Michilimackinac I would be living on Jacques's farm. If I married James, Oakbridge would one day belong to James and me. The carriage carried me between ancient oak trees that guarded either side of the driveway. Beneath the oaks, gillyflowers and bluebells were blooming. The green fields were dotted with sheep whose names I now knew: Devon and Oxford and Shropshire sheep. As I looked out at it all, I wondered if I could be happy here.

CHAPTER
15

ON MY RETURN Angelique had pleasant news. The Cunninghams had come to dinner and all had gone well. "Except," Angelique said, "Mrs. Cunningham rearranged the furniture, criticized the soup, and told me I was eating too much of one thing and not enough of another." There was much giggling over this, for what would have been gall and wormwood under the Cunninghams' roof did not bother Angelique in the least now that she had her own home.

"It's your turn," Angelique said. "I want to hear everything about your visit."

I hardly knew where to begin. "The whole island of Michilimackinac would fit into their estate," I told her. "Yet they were so kind to me, giving me a horse to ride, and letting me scold them about Ireland. They have a milkmaid who does nothing all day long but cool and cream the milk. And imagine having so much property you could get lost on it, as James and I did one day."

I told her everything except James's proposal and my talk with his mother. Although those things were always in my mind, I could not bring myself to say them aloud. It was only after I had told every last detail of my visit to Castle Oakbridge that Angelique thought to say, "There is a letter for you, Mary. It came just after you left."

I recognized White Hawk's writing and carried the letter to my room to read. Holding the very envelope he had held, I felt I had somehow betrayed White Hawk. I had been thinking of exchanging Michilimackinac for Castle Oakbridge. Yet, with White Hawk's letter in my hand, my heart was going as fast as a rabbit chased by a fox. I could not sort out my feelings.

As I opened the letter I believed it would tell me of White Hawk's decision to stay on in Detroit or to return to L'Arbre Croche. Instead the letter sent me flying to Angelique.

April 30, 1817
Michilimackinac

Dear Mary,

Your father has begged me not to write to you, but I believe you would never forgive me if I did not tell you what has happened. I am sending this letter with the first sloop to leave the island this spring.

I am sure you have guessed from his letters that Jacques has been unhappy working for Mr. Astor in his fur business. Two weeks ago Jacques had some sort of argument with the man who employed him, and resigned his job. After that he spent most of his time talking with the traders who come to the island to bring their pelts. As you well know, he was never much good at working on the farm, so your father has had to do everything for himself.

Little Cloud helped with the work, but she is expecting a baby. Although she liked the island it was not her home and she missed her family. She wanted to be with her tribe when the baby was born.

Two weeks ago Jacques and Little Cloud suddenly left with some fur traders. They will not return until next spring. This was a great blow to your father, but had he been in good health he still could have managed the farm.

Now, Mary, I come to the sad part. Your father is not well. This happened after Jacques had left or I am sure he would never have gone away. The MacNeils, the Sinclairs, and the Wests have all tried to help your father. When I am on the island from L'Arbre Croche I lend a hand as well. Your father will be angry that I have written, but I feel sure you would want to know.

You will have guessed that for my own part I have decided to leave Detroit and come back to my people. However happy it would make your father (and me, Mary!) to have you back, you must decide the best course for yourself.

Your good friend,
White Hawk

June 15, 1817
St. John's Wood

My dear papa,

I am coming home at once.

All my love,
Mary

June 15, 1817
St. John's Wood

Dear James,

I am in a great rush. Next week I sail for home on the British merchant ship the Otter. I hardly know what to say. My papa is sick and all alone, for my brother and his wife have left the island. I cannot blame my brother, for he never asked for the farm, but only to be left to his adventures. I must go to Papa at once. It is over six weeks since the letter was written and it will be another two months before I am home. I cannot waste a day.

You must know how sorry I am to leave

*without seeing you and thanking your parents
again for their kindness. When I am back on
the island I know Castle Oakbridge will seem a
dream. But I shall hold on to the dream and not
let it go. I pray that we will see one another
again.*

> *God bless you,*
> *Mary*

There was no answer to my letter to James. I
hoped he was not angry with me for leaving so
suddenly. I did not blame him for his anger, but
I was very hurt not to have had at least a word
from him.

I could hardly bear to part with Angelique.
We clung to one another and nearly flooded the
room with our tears. "If it weren't for Daniel and
the baby coming," Angelique said, "I would go
with you, Mary. Please give my love to Papa and
write me the minute you get back to the island.
When you see Jacques and Little Cloud you
must tell them that one day our children must
meet as cousins."

Daniel went with me in the coach to
Portsmouth, where I was to board the *Otter*. As
we entered the town I thought of how much had

happened since I had landed there on the *Comfort*. When I had first come to England I had thought only of how I longed to return to the island. All of my heart was on Michilimackinac. Now that was changed. There were two islands in my heart, each one precious to me. But if I had one, I could not have the other. I felt as though I would spend the rest of my life cut in two. I did not see how I could ever leave Papa and make such a long trip again.

I bid farewell to Daniel and climbed into the boat that would carry me out to the *Otter*. I was impatient to reach the ship and begin my journey back to Papa and my island of Michilimackinac, yet I could not stop myself from looking back and waving to Daniel, who was growing smaller and smaller on the shore of that other island where I was leaving Angelique—and James—behind.

Captain Bing received me as I clambered onto the deck of the *Otter*. He welcomed me on board, explaining that I would be sharing a cabin with two other women. Because the *Otter* was only a merchant ship and not a ship belonging to the Royal Navy, the captain was not so splendidly dressed as Captain Hodge had been. He appeared cross, and turned from me to call to one of the crew who was hauling at the anchor. "Look lively, there. You'll have to move faster than that if you want a berth on this ship. That may have been your style on His Majesty's ship, but we're less spit and polish and more plain work here."

I saw the young man renew his efforts. As I looked again, I saw that it was James. I would have exclaimed aloud but the slightest flicker of his eye warned me that such a show of recognition would not go well for him with Captain Bing. With the greatest difficulty I kept silent and allowed one of the ship's officers to show me to my cabin. Although I followed the man down the ladder, all my thoughts remained on deck with James.

I was so flustered, I could hardly put a foot right, and stumbled. The officer urged, "One hand for yourself, miss, the other for the ship." The words that Mr. Rachert had once said to me took me back to my early days on the *Comfort* and my first meeting with James. Did James mean to follow me all the way home to Michilimackinac? I could not believe that it was just an accident that he was on the very boat I was taking home. In my amazement I couldn't decide if I was pleased. My thoughts were all taken up with the worries I had over Papa. I could find no room to puzzle out how I felt about James.

My own confusion disappeared the moment I entered my cabin. I had never seen such upheaval. The three bunks inside the tiny room were covered with clothes. Trunks and boxes of every kind were strewn about the floor, so there was no space to turn around. On one of the bunks a heap of clothes shuddered and shook. I saw that it was a girl of my age. She was crying and moaning. A woman went to her, flinging her arms around the girl. "Charlotte, you must be brave. You must bear up." Then the woman turned to me. "I am Mrs. Limpet and this is my daughter, Charlotte. Poor Charlotte suffers terribly from seasickness. Even the sight of a boat makes her ill. I would never allow this torment, but Mr. Limpet was sent to England by President Monroe, and I could not let him travel alone to a foreign country. You take your life in your hands with foreigners. And the English do not know how to feed a man. I had to see to everything. I could not leave him for a minute. Now he has kindly insisted on our returning home ahead of him. He thinks only of our welfare. But the trip will be a torture to Charlotte." She gave me a quick look. "I hope you have very little luggage, for the cabin is impossibly small and we have hardly any room for our trunks."

When she paused for a breath I hastily said, "I only need a few things. My trunk can go down into the hold. Perhaps the voyage will be smooth and your daughter will not be troubled."

"Oh, there can be no question of smoothness. The least motion brings on her sickness."

And indeed, though the *Otter* was only shifting in her berth, Charlotte was looking very green. A moment later she was sick. There was no time to worry about James, for the Limpets took all of my attention.

It was the next morning when there was a quick knock at the cabin door. Mrs. Limpet opened the door and there was James with a note in his hand. "What do you want?" she asked crossly.

"Captain's compliments, mam, and I have a message for Miss O'Shea."

In a haughty voice Mrs. Limpet said, "Give it here, young man, and get about your work."

"My instructions are to give it directly to Miss O'Shea."

"Nonsense." She snatched the note from a protesting James and slammed the door in his face.

Not to be outdone in discourtesy, I snatched

the note from Mrs. Limpet, who was about to read it.

"Well!" she said. "I am sure your mother would want me to read any messages you receive to be sure they are proper. I don't trust that young man at all. He had a forward look. These sailors are all the very lowest class. I think poorly of the captain that he did not send an officer with his message."

"I found the men aboard the ship on which I sailed to England all gentlemen—whatever their background." I had to bite my tongue to keep from pointing out that she had snatched the note from the hand of a duke's son.

Charlotte raised herself from her cot to ask, "Aren't you going to read the note and tell us what is in it? I am sure Mama is right. We ought to know what it says."

Mrs. Limpet stared at me. "I wonder that the captain should trouble himself by writing to you. Perhaps he has sent the note to tell you that you ought not to be in our cabin at all. You make it very crowded here."

I only replied, "It is very stuffy, as well. I'm going above for some air."

I escaped their suspicious stares and made my way up the ladder to a secluded spot on the deck and eagerly read James's note.

My dear Mary,

Please do not think that I am pursuing you. I know that you are troubled by your father's illness and can only think of reaching your home as soon as possible. I will leave the ship in New York and while you travel to your island I will make my way to the West. I have long desired to see your wild forests and mountains and the Indians who make their home there. I want to paint it all before your settlers spread over the land and make of America another England.

When I learned you were sailing on this ship I applied for a berth so that I might at least catch a glimpse of you for a few more weeks. When you leave the ship and begin your travels to your home, my heart will go with you. I would do whatever I could to make you happy.

Please think of me sometimes. When I have had my fill of the wilderness I will come to your island and ask again, Mary, that you be my wife. God willing we will travel together back to Oakbridge and a happy life.

With all of my love,
James

My hands were trembling. I longed to run to him but I knew it was impossible. I had seen at once that Captain Bing was a hard master—not because it made for an orderly ship, but because he enjoyed using his power over his men. Any effort I made to seek James out would only cause trouble for him with the captain. But it was not only that. I felt no matter what James said in his letter, he still had hopes I could give him an answer that would please him. How could I give him an answer when I did not know my own mind? Slowly I dragged myself back to the cabin before Mrs. Limpet should be suspicious about my absence.

And, indeed, she already was. She greeted me with a frown. "Mary, I think I must speak with the captain about sending so vulgar a seaman to us with messages. His doing so is an affront to our dignity and it is not fitting that we should have to converse with such low people."

Before I could think of some way to stop her, there was a knock on the door and our breakfast trays were carried in. I breathed a sigh of relief, but I knew I would have to think quickly to keep her mind from James. Mrs. Limpet had a hearty appetite, but Charlotte as usual turned away from her meal. While Mrs. Limpet begged her daughter to try a bit of food I began to make a fuss about spooning something from my soup.

Mrs. Limpet noticed. "What are you about, Mary?"

"It is nothing," I said, crunching some imaginary thing with my spoon. "It is only some cockroaches that were floating in my soup."

Mrs. Limpet screamed and Charlotte lunged for the bowl she kept by her bedside. After that there was no more talk of speaking with the captain about anything but what was to be found in the soup.

We sailed into New York Harbor on a bright July day. As sad as my homecoming was, my heart leapt at the sight of my own dear country. The Limpets hastened from the boat with barely a civil good-bye to me. Though I was anxious to begin my journey to the island and Papa, I dawdled a bit in my leaving, determined to speak some word of farewell to James. While the passengers were free to go, the crew had to remain aboard for several days readying the ship for its return voyage. James and I had exchanged many secret looks on the voyage but there had been no chance for words.

My trunk was already on the barge that was to

take me ashore, and I was about to follow it when I felt a push. Startled, I looked up to see James trying not to grin. "Look alive, there, sailor!" an officer shouted at him. "One more clumsy move like that and the lash will give you a lesson in behavior." James quickly disappeared into the crowd of sailors emptying the hold of the ship's cargo.

It was only after I was in the barge and reaching for a handkerchief to wipe away the sea spray that I felt it—an object wrapped around with a piece of paper, which James must have slipped into my pocket when he bumped into me. I made myself wait until I was on shore and alone for a moment before I drew it out. I held in my hand a gold brooch in the shape of a spray of forget-me-nots. It was elegantly made, the flowers fashioned of sapphires, the leaves of emeralds. I was sure I could not accept so valuable a gift, but there was no way to return it. Only a few words were scrawled on the note: *Mary, don't forget me.*

CHAPTER

16

THOUGH IN TRUTH the journey back to the island was faster than my trip to England had been, I thought it would never end. Lake Ontario and Lake Huron seemed like endless stretches of water, wider than all the seas put together. Yet when I finally saw my green island in the distance I wished the journey to go on forever, for I was afraid of what I would find. What would I do if something had happened to Papa? I could not imagine life without him. Even while

I was far away in England he was always with me in my thoughts.

As we sailed into the harbor, I saw a hundred landmarks. I could see the bundle of houses along Main Street, the steeple of St. Anne's Church, the Indian teepees along the shore. Watching over it all stood Fort Michilimackinac, flying the American flag.

The moment the sloop touched the wharf I hiked up my skirts and leapt onto shore. Without waiting for my trunk I flew past the crowds of traders putting in winter supplies, past the Indian camp, across Main Street and up the hill. Every tree and stone on the path was familiar and dear to me. It was the path Angelique, Jacques, and I had taken hundreds of times. It was where we slid down the hill on a winter's day, and where White Hawk had told me he would fight with the British against us. The wild asters and goldenrod were blooming just as they were when Angelique, a wreath of wild roses in her hair, walked to St. Anne's for her wedding.

My hair was flying, a heel was off one of my boots, and I had ripped my skirt on a blackberry briar, but I stopped for nothing. At last I saw the farm, and there, sitting on a bench, was Papa. I was hidden by a tree, so I saw him before he saw me. I held back for a moment, taken aback by Papa's appearance. He was thinner, and though the late August sun was warm he was wrapped in heavy clothing against some chill that had nothing to do with weather. It made me shiver. I did not see how I could have left him all these months.

I hurried toward Papa and flung my arms around him. He had always been so strong. Now there seemed so little to hold in my arms. Both our faces were wet with tears.

"Mary," he said, "I thought I would never see you again." He looked hard at me. "You are a young lady now. After London your old home will seem a sorry comedown. You won't find any dukes or duchesses here." There was a peevish note to his voice I had never heard before.

Perhaps he had thought I had been boasting when I had written about James's parents. I had only meant to amuse Papa. Now I wished with all my heart I had never said a word about dukes and duchesses. I forced myself to sound cheerful. "Oh, Papa, this is the best place in the world. It is better than any great castle you could find in England. And, Papa, when the duke spoke against Ireland I stuck up for her."

At last Papa smiled. "That's my girl. And you

must tell me all about Angelique and Daniel. To think Angelique is expecting a child and I will never see it. But first come inside and rest. You are surely tired from your long journey."

As I followed Papa into the cabin I tried hard not to let him see my disappointment. The bed was unmade, the dishes unwashed, and the floor unswept. Mice peeked out of the corners and ants climbed the table leg.

Papa said, "I had thought to have things looking better for you, but the farm has become too much for me."

"Never mind, I'll soon have it tidied up." After I gave Papa all the news about England, I said, "Now you must tell me about Jacques and Little Cloud and all of our friends." I settled at his feet with my head against his knee, as I used to, and took his cold hand in mine to warm it.

Papa sighed. "I have been unfair to Jacques and to you, Mary. I should never have forced Jacques to stay here on the island when he longed to be free to travel west. I have changed my will, Mary. The farm will be yours. Jacques agrees that it should be so. But I want you to promise me that you will not stay here if you would rather return to England. If you think the farm is too much for you or you cannot be content on the island, you must sell the farm and go where you will be happy. Promise me that, Mary."

"I'll promise anything to make you happy, Papa, but now that I'm home I'll never want to leave the island again. The farm is the dearest place in the world. It means everything to me and I'll soon have it right again."

Later, while Papa was resting, I slipped outside. I had said that I would soon have the farm right again but I did not see how I could keep that promise. The garden was rank with weeds. The corn in the field should have been harvested weeks ago. There was a hole in the fence around the chicken coop. At my every step there was an explosion of feathers as runaway chickens flew up. The barn had not been mucked out and Belle and George looked scrawny. I put my arms around Belle's warm, smooth coat, as I had done so often before, and sobbed.

It was there Dr. West found me. "Great heavens, Mary! What a surprise! But what are these tears?"

"Dr. West, Papa looks so ill and the farm is so run-down, I don't see how I am to fix it by myself."

Dr. West shook his head. "It has been too much for your father. He tries, but he's not strong enough. We have attempted to do the work for him, but he is too proud for that. There is nothing for it but to sell the farm, Mary. It would not bring a great deal, but enough to keep you modestly."

"I could not bear to give up the farm, Dr. West," I told him, my voice nearly breaking. "Besides, it would kill Papa to sell it."

"There is no question of that, Mary. I give your father no more than a few weeks to live. His heart is very weak. It kept beating only because of his wish to see you before he died. Now that his dearest wish has been granted I think he will soon pass away."

He stopped when he saw the look on my face. "I am sorry to be so blunt, Mary. I know it is a sad homecoming for you, but it is best that I am honest so that you can make plans for your departure."

"I don't want to depart. I want to stay right here. And I don't know how you can be so sure that Papa will die." Yet even as I protested I felt Dr. West was right.

"I truly hope I am wrong, but everything I know about medicine tells me your father's days are limited. Come, I see I have been too abrupt. We must take one day at a time. Mrs. West and the girls will be over as soon as I tell them you are here."

Indeed they came at once, bringing cakes and jellies and baskets of vegetables and fruit. I was welcomed home warmly and a nourishing bowl of soup was presented to Papa. Then I was taken aside and questioned closely about London. What was the latest fashion in clothes? How were the tables set? What food was served and how? What were the latest dances? "I suppose Angelique lives simply?" Elizabeth wanted to know.

"Oh, yes. They have a small house in a distant corner of London."

"So she does not go much into society?"

"She and Daniel are very happy to keep to themselves."

"If I were in London I would not go a single evening without attending a party," Elizabeth said. "It must have been dull for you just to sit about and never meet anyone."

"Oh, I met some very pleasant people," I said. "But you know me. I am only a country girl." Mrs. West gave me a sharp look. I believe she had some idea I was ragging her but I looked very innocent. It gave me more pleasure to keep my castle and James and the duke and duchess to myself than it would have to hand them over to Elizabeth.

All this time I could see that Emma was paying little attention to her mother's and sister's questions. Now with a blushing face she asked, "What do you hear from Jacques," adding quickly, "and Little Cloud?"

"Papa says Jacques has promised to come before the winter. I am sure Little Cloud and the baby will come as well."

Emma seemed pleased at the news, though I knew her pleasure was in seeing Jacques and not his wife and baby.

No sooner had the Wests taken their leave than Pere Mercier appeared, huffing and puffing from the climb up the bluff. I noticed that he walked now with a slight limp and his face, tanned from fishing, had many new wrinkles. With Pere Mercier there was no pretending. He did not want to know about the latest fashions in cassocks and church services. Instead he took my hands in his. "I know you are worried about your dear papa, Mary. I only wish your homecoming could have been a happier one."

"I know how ill Papa is, but even allowing for the illness he does not seem himself."

"He worries about what will happen to the

farm after he is gone. He knows that Jacques will never stay in one place. Angelique is across the sea. He worries about you having to manage on your own. I tell you this, Mary, because I want you to understand why your father is unhappy. I don't tell you to make you stay here. We all think the farm would be too much for you. And believe me, even losing the farm would not hurt your father as much as knowing you were keeping it just for his sake when you wished to be elsewhere."

"Pere Mercier, I want to stay on the farm more than anything in the world, and I mean to do it." I took a deep breath. "Alone, if I have to."

He looked into my face for a long time. "I know you mean that, Mary. But you'll need help. I'll see to that."

And he did. The next day as I was getting Papa's breakfast we heard wagons and many voices. The MacNeils, the Sinclairs, Pere Mercier, and the Wests were all there. They came armed with pitchforks and shovels. They were all dressed in rough clothes and the women wore sunbonnets. I hurried out. Papa was only a few steps behind me.

"Here is my work crew," Pere Mercier said.

There was much embracing and tears as I

exchanged greetings with our old friends. Papa was overwhelmed and had to be settled on the porch while the others went to work. At first he protested that he must do the work himself and not depend on others, but I said we must not hurt the feelings of our kind neighbors by sending them away when they meant well. Reluctantly Papa agreed.

Mrs. Sinclair marched into the garden and attacked the weeds with her hoe. Mr. Sinclair and Mr. MacNeil began harvesting the corn. Pere Mercier hitched up his cassock. Pulling a horrified Elizabeth and Emma after him, he moved into the stables with a shovel. Dr. West started to repair the chicken fence. Mrs. West and Mrs. MacNeil, with scrub brushes and dust cloths, headed for our cabin. I was everywhere at once, gathering up the chickens, soothing Belle and George, bringing water from the spring for the hot, thirsty workers, cleaning Elizabeth's shoes, and calming Papa. He was more cheerful now, smiling and shaking his head at all the bustle around him.

It was long after noon when we all gathered about our table to enjoy one of Mr. MacNeil's famous smoked hams and Mrs. Sinclair's beans baked in maple syrup and Mrs. West's princess cake. Papa joined us and for a short while looked just as he used to. Our talk was cheerful. Mrs. MacNeil said blackberries had never been so plentiful. Mrs. West told me that Mr. Astor's American Fur Company was bringing new people to the island, many of them "quite civilized." Elizabeth named the officers at the fort who were both handsome and unmarried. As soon as I dared I asked the Sinclairs how White Hawk was.

"He is at L'Arbre Croche," Mr. Sinclair told me.

Mrs. Sinclair added with a smile, "But he often comes to visit us."

I rejoiced in the thought that White Hawk was so close and that any day I might see him. I wondered if in the year I had been away he had changed. Perhaps he now cared for some young woman in his tribe at L'Arbre Croche. His letter said he would be happy to see me back, but maybe only as a friend. If he had found someone else I could not be angry with him, for hadn't I thought of marrying James?

By evening, when the wagons had rolled away, the farm and the cabin were nearly as good as new. But I knew I could not depend upon such a day again. Our dear neighbors would be willing to help, but they had their own duties. I had a lifetime of hard work ahead of me. I thought of James and how different my life would be if I were to choose to spend it with him. I would only have to raise a finger and there would be a servant to wait upon me. But I did not see how I could move Castle Oakbridge across the sea, and I could not bear to leave Michilimackinac again.

Like the waves that lapped against the island shore, one day followed another. I was up before sunrise and at work until sunset. In the evenings I listened to Papa, who spoke more and more of his childhood in Ireland. Often now he mentioned my mother as if he was soon to see her. And each day he grew a little weaker.

One evening he asked me to help him to a place on the farm where he could look out at the two great lakes that wreathe around our island. He spoke of the day when he and my mother first came to the island with Jacques and Angelique. I had other thoughts. Soon Jacques would be returning with Little Cloud and their baby. White Hawk would come as well—for the Sinclairs had heard that he was on his way from L'Arbre Croche. And James? One day James might also sail across the lakes to Michilimackinac. Together Papa and I talked of the seasons on the island, the winter when the island was a great white hump nearly buried in snow, the spring when the gulls came flying back, the summers with their shining blue waters and soft winds and the sound of the Indian drums on the shore.

As I listened to his words, I could feel that everything was going to be all right. For now I still had Papa. And even with all the hard work, I knew that the island was where I belonged. I was home.